Passing Through a Prairie Country

ALSO BY DENNIS E. STAPLES

This Town Sleeps

Passing Through
a Prairie Country

A Novel

Dennis E. Staples

Counterpoint † California

Passing Through a Prairie Country

This is a work of fiction. All of the characters, organizations, and events portrayed in this novel are either products of the author's imagination or are used fictitiously.

First Counterpoint edition: 2025

Library of Congress Cataloging-in-Publication Data
Names: Staples, Dennis E., author.
Title: Passing through a prairie country : a novel / Dennis E. Staples.
Description: First Counterpoint edition. | California : Counterpoint, 2025.
Identifiers: LCCN 2024043764 | ISBN 9781640096875 (hardcover) | ISBN
    9781640096882 (ebook)
Subjects: LCGFT: Thrillers (Fiction) | Novels.
Classification: LCC PS3619.T3675 P37 2025 | DDC 813/.6—dc23/eng/20240920
LC record available at https://lccn.loc.gov/2024043764

Jacket design and illustration by Nicole Caputo
Eyes © iStock / Chartchai Sansaneeyashewin
Book design by Laura Berry
Skull © Adobe Stock / ars

COUNTERPOINT
San Francisco and Los Angeles, CA
www.counterpointpress.com

Printed in the United States of America

10 9 8 7 6 5 4 3 2 1

For Jesse and Rob

You doubt the tale? ah, you will understand;
For, as men muse upon that fable old,
They give sad credence always at the last,
However they have caviled at its truth,
When with a tear-dimmed vision they behold,
Swift sinking in the ocean of the Past,
The lovely lost Atlantis of their Youth.

—ELLA WHEELER WILCOX,
The Lost Land

The Ojibway believes his home after death to lie west-
ward . . . the road of souls is sometimes called Ke-wa-
kun-ah: Homeward Road. This road is represented as
passing mostly through a prairie country.

—WILLIAM W. WARREN,
A History of the Ojibway People

And now that their merry pageant seems to have
reached its peak, I think the time is right to awaken
this mob from its hypnotic slumber and thrill the day-
lights out of them.

—THOMAS LIGOTTI,
"Drink to Me Only with Labyrinthine Eyes"

Passing Through a Prairie Country

Prologue KENO ROAD

November 1, 2017

O l' Froglegs Bullhead lived in a small public housing unit with a CNA in one of the unincorporated communities between two cities, Waubajeeg and Indian Hollow, on the Languille Lake Reservation in northern Minnesota. At fifty-eight years old, Ol' Froglegs was wheelchair-bound; a work accident had taken his left leg at thirty-five, and neglect for his health had taken his right foot at fifty.

But insistent on a certain amount of independence, Froglegs wheeled himself the five miles south to Waubajeeg whenever he had extra income to put in the slots, or sometimes he just grabbed a bite to eat at the food court and shot the breeze with his numerous friends and cousins who worked, lived, or played—or some combination of those—at Hidden Atlantis Lake Resort and Casino. Though a troubled soul in his youth, with dozens of bridges burned behind him, he'd spent the last decade of his life trying to rebuild any and every relationship he could.

He wheeled into the back entrance of the casino in the afternoon, scaring a flock of white pigeons from the sidewalk.

He was delighted to see one of his great-nieces was working at the security counter. She greeted him with a big, beaming smile. It was always nice seeing a family member with a full set of teeth, unlike himself.

On this day, he drew nine hundred dollars from the ATM near the keno machines, but he couldn't find an open one to play. So he rolled over to an electronic poker game and tried his luck with virtual cards. A half hour and a hundred dollars later, he grew bored of poker and instead went to the front entrance to chat with the young bucks at the security office.

He held up two fists in a playful taunt. "I bet all my money that I can take all of you savs, right here, right now."

"Let's go then," said his favorite great-niece, Cherie. "I'll knock all your teeth out, gramps."

"Oh, fuck you," Ol' Froglegs said with a gummy laugh. "I should knock some of yours loose for saying that."

Cherie walked forward and held her arms up. "Okay. Let's throw down, you froggy fuck." Instead of punching him, she lowered her outstretched arms and hugged him. "You winning big yet?"

"Nah. I'm not going back out there until y'all turn the machines up."

"Sorry, guy. All the big wins were probably yesterday."

It was the day after Halloween. Froglegs hadn't been able to make it down the road to play because of a sudden snowstorm that melted away by evening.

"Then tell me which machines are still hot." He pulled out a twenty-dollar bill and held it to her. "Is this one lucky?"

Cherie laughed. "I'm not Lady Luck, uncle."

"What about Alana? Where's her ugly mug right now?"

"It's her day off. And she'd slap you if she heard that, ya know."

He sighed. "Guess it's not my lucky day then. Maybe I'll come back late tonight and try the high-stakes machines."

"I'll see you then, uncle."

"Hey, when's the next drawing, my girl?"

"New year, right at midnight, uncle. Ain't that past your bedtime?"

"Your uncle ain't got no bedtime," he said as he rolled away.

Ol' Froglegs played thirty more dollars on a nickel keno machine, but he slowly lost it all as the numbers came in. It looked like Lady Luck was sleeping in, after partying herself out on Halloween. He slammed his Styrofoam cup of coffee and made for the back entrance again.

"I'll be back," he said to the new guard, a timid-looking white girl no older than twenty-five. "Save me a jackpot or two."

"Have a nice day, sir," came the nervous reply.

He wheeled himself out on the paved walking path that ran parallel to Jackson Lane, all the way up to Indian Hollow, where it ended at a cozy park. The hardest part of the trip was a mile away from the casino, where the trail hit a slow and steady incline and always gave him a good workout.

When he reached the top, he could see a gathering of people walking toward him in the distance. At first it looked like they were in one big group on the walking path, but then he noticed more were gathered in the ditch between the path and the road. Some were beating the ground with their fists, but others simply drifted back and forth, their heads nodding up and down.

Froglegs wondered if this was a group of people who had just been to a methadone or Suboxone clinic. He remembered vividly the time in his life when he'd had to rely on those things to function. He looked on the crowd with recognition and pity.

But as they got closer, one of them, a young Ojibwe man, disappeared like candle smoke. His body became a thin, snaking wisp of fog. Others faded in and out of view. Some twitched and convulsed like spiders who'd cruelly had several legs removed by wayward children.

The breath left his throat. There was a small road a few yards ahead and to the right, and without much thought, he wheeled himself off the paved trail and into the woods. A half mile in, he remembered that this was the location of a cemetery. In the distance, beyond the barren autumn trees, he could see the shape of Hidden Atlantis, with its bright gold and baby-blue trim on the exterior walls, and the three vibrant slides of the water park. He stopped a few feet from the entrance to catch his breath.

"Give us the cash."

It was a man's voice behind him, though still fairly young. He turned around, and on the trail he'd come in through, there were three Ojibwe men, probably no older than twenty. They wore loose black clothing and red bandannas over their mouths. The one who'd spoken held a metal bat in his hand.

"Now. All of it."

"I ain't got no cash, you little assholes."

"Bullshit. We saw you leave the casino."

"Doesn't mean I have money. I lost it all. Don't you know how a casino works?"

"Have it your way, then, old man."

The boys rushed at him, and he raised his arms in front of his face. The bat hit his arm, and the other two boys knocked him to the ground. He tumbled from his wheelchair and landed face down on the ground. He wanted to fight back, but there was little he could do. The bat smacked his shoulders and back over and over until the pain overtook his body and sent him into shock.

He turned his head back to the trail, and just before all went dark, the apparitions he'd seen on the road passed by, stumbling toward the casino. The boys took the money from his wallet and ran further into the trees.

PART ONE

Hidden Atlantis

"No," said Lizzie, "No, no, no;
Their offers should not charm us,
Their evil gifts would harm us."
She thrust a dimpled finger
In each ear, shut eyes and ran;
Curious Laura chose to linger
Wondering at each merchant man.

—CHRISTINA ROSSETTI, *Goblin Market*

Chapter 1 ♧ ROLLING HOME

MARION LAFOURNIER

November 10, 2017

I used to think it was a long drive from Languille Lake to the Twin Cities. I once had a coworker in an office who said he used to commute there every morning and the only things that made it bearable were his plentiful batches of weed cookies and an Altoids can full of joints. Seemed impossible then, but now it feels more necessary than proof of insurance for any trip longer than three hours.

I spent the last week offloading most of my heavier furniture to any friends who would take it, so the car is packed with a suitcase of clothes, a few electronics, a box or two of miscellaneous trinkets, a seatbelt-cutter and window-breaker pocketknife (at my stepfather's insistence), two tall energy drinks, and six fat rolled joints in an Altoids can. The wintergreen smell is long gone.

These supplies are for the trip down to a new home in Minneapolis, which I rented from one of my aunts. I sold my place in Half Lake to an ex-something, Shannon. He's still fragile about our end and endlessly unsure about coming out of the closet. When I hand him the keys to his new house, there's not much to say as I leave. For Shannon's sake, I hold back a few tears as I pet my dog, Basil, now also his. If Shannon sees me cry, he might start again. But there's just no room on my schedule for a man's tears today.

"Love you, pup."

He gives me one last wide dog smile, and then Shannon brings him inside without a word.

South of Geshig about twenty-five miles, after passing through Walker and coming to Waubajeeg, I stop at the Hidden Atlantis Casino. Can't help myself. The minute I left town, I lit up a joint and downed the first energy drink. Now I really need to piss.

When I turn into the parking lot, I narrowly miss hitting a flock of pale birds. They'd been pecking at a basket of French fries in the road and didn't appreciate the disturbance.

Along the sidewalk into the building, a group of cedar bushes shakes in the early winter wind. A few have faded orange branches; one is so dry and lifeless it breaks off the tree and falls in my path.

The same moment I walk through the second set of doors and onto the matte, rosy tiles of the casino entryway, a lanky security guard is escorting a young Native guy outside.

"How many times are we gonna do this, Liam?" the security guard says.

"You coulda just looked the other way, brother," the young man says.

"Consider me not getting the tribal cops involved me 'looking the other way.'"

The guard lets go of Liam's shoulder and places his hands on his belt above his hips, his eyes sharp and cold.

"Hey, *niij*," Liam says as he passes me at the door. "You got a dollar?"

"Go."

At the guard's stern voice, Liam ducks out without another word.

"Sorry about that, bud," the guard says to me. He has a pale blond crew cut and a stoic demeanor. "Just lookin' out fer ya." He shrugs and strides away before I can respond.

I hang my coat on a hook near the entrance and head straight for the restroom after greeting the host. I haven't been in this casino since I was eighteen, right before my grandmother Eunice died. She and Hazel had worked out their issues, at least to the extent that they could be worked out, and we lived with her for fifteen years.

In her last few months, she was frail and wheelchair-bound, but the moment we passed through the front doors and saw the rainbow of electric lights on the machines, her spirits lifted. She taught me how to use the slot machines, what lines and bets meant, and how to rub the screen as the reels spun to trigger the bonus game. All those old-fashioned casino superstitions.

I still see patrons trying this as I walk through the gold-and-blue-lined walls of Hidden Atlantis. Some are falling asleep in their seats. Some are visibly tweaking. Others chain-smoke cheap cigarettes and stare as their money spins down to zero.

Even so, there's still a lot more smiles than frowns in the glittering crowd. It could be worth playing a few dollars.

I walk to the gift shop to break a twenty and get some smaller bills for playing. The walls of the gift shop are ocean-blue stained glass and give the impression of being inside a large aquarium. Small pearlescent shapes of plastic fish and bubbles bob up and down on the glass in wavy lines.

Gifts sit atop a cerulean Formica table on the opposite end

of the cashier's counter. It's filled with an array of Indigenous-style arts and crafts: intricately netted dreamcatchers on woolly staffs in shapes of tipis, God's eyes, and even head-dresses. Jewelry, T-shirts, lanyards, and beaded pocket lighter holders adorned with the shapes and colors of the standard medicine wheel. Almost all are wrapped with shiny black leather binding. I remember seeing the other boys in school scratch at their baseball gloves or boots to see if they were real leather, but I never learned what to look for or know if that method was effective. Some of the tags on the trinkets claim authenticity and natural materials, but it wouldn't sur-prise me if it were all some lab-spun sinew that'll be ruled cancerous in California someday.

The shop snacks are vending machine quality, and there are complimentary soda fountains across the casino floor, so their drink selection is limited to energy drinks and coffee. All the alcohol is at the bar, where the big winners go to brag about their haul and leave tips only a shkweb'd-up person could give.

On a rack holding velvet quilts with geometric patterns and small birch-bark boxes, a packaged item catches my eye. The three bundles of plants inside the plastic are familiar to any Indian. A roll of sage, a braid of sweetgrass, and a cluster of cedar branches.

A gold label with dark laurels on the front says SACRED HERBS, 3-VARIETY PACK. It's only $4.99.

Something about seeing those sacred herbs, and maybe the burst of a stale smell from the casino, makes me want a pack of cigarettes.

I grab the herbs from the rack. When I look up, there's an old man staring at me through the glass from outside the gift shop. He laughs when he sees how startled I am. He mouths something I can't hear, but it looks like "good choice." I turn around without acknowledging him and pay for my shit at the counter. A young woman, who is also nodding off, not unlike the slot machine patrons, drowses her way through the transaction. Her eyes are barely open when she gives me the change, a few vibrant copper pennies, a dingy nickel, and a quarter covered in a rosy-orange paint. She mumbles, "Thank you for choosing Hidden Atlantis," and I leave without a word. When I look back, she's sleeping. In the distance, a gaggle of security guards laugh at her, and one walks over to shake her awake.

I stop outside the gift shop entrance to open my cigarettes and check my phone, but to my right, I notice that old man from the window coming my way. He's got a friendly smile that looks like he wants to talk, so I turn away without a word and keep walking. I glance back when I'm beyond one of the slot machine banks and see him inside the shop's fish-tank walls.

The casino's mix of lights and electronic sounds and music from the speakers of the machine banks makes for a loud but calming atmosphere. Far different than when I was a kid on the rez and we hated the casinos because of how much time and money our parents spent here. It seemed unimaginable then, but there's something appealing about wandering for hours, hearing the excited voices win, the angry voices lose, and the constant clacking of buttons.

I send a quick text to my mother, Hazel. If she were here, she'd show me exactly where to go and what machines to use. Some machines pay out better than others, and that one does this, and this one does that. Some have animations; some are high-yield progressives; some are nickel and penny machines. There are faces of geishas, tigers, Egyptian royalty and gods, animals, and some licensed movie versions like old pinball machines. Nothing feels right, though, so by the time I check my phone again, I've wandered around here for twenty minutes and still haven't lost any money. The signal struggles, but eventually it pulls through and shows my mom's reply.

Not sure what pays good but try the one with the baby penguins. I like that one.

Thanks, Mom.

The security guards might get suspicious if I keep this up. I grab a cup of soda from the fountain and beeline it to a machine bank. The game is called *Green Gardens*. The chair is a faded maroon vinyl with spiderweb fissures running across the backrest. Five dollars disappears from my hand into the machine. I play the lowest bet.

I can't imagine a more infuriating way to pass time. I put in another dollar. After I lose it, I walk around a bit more and find the baby penguin machine my mom mentioned, a tall neon-screened cartoon game that features penguins sliding on their bellies over the snow as the bonus animation. The title is *Pesky Penguins*. Ten dollars later, I'm unable to trigger the animation.

This is such a waste of money, I text.

Try keno? Heard of people winning big there.

Will do.

If your playing slots should I tell Aunt Gwen you'll be delayed?

Sure. Thanks! Will let you know if I hit a jackpot.

A minute or so later, I spot the keno section: five tall banks clustered around the center of the casino floor. From this part of the floor, you can see the full view of the circular mural on the ceiling, a pantheon of gods with a teal-tailed Poseidon near the center, his trident pointed to a warm sun lamp. All the other chairs on this bank are filled, and the man I sit next to lets me know it. A vibrant plastic placard above the screen reads KING TUT'S KENO.

"Got the beginner's luck, eh?" he says with a scoff. He's a Native guy, maybe early middle age based on the sparse white whiskers on his lips and chin.

"Huh? I haven't even played yet."

"Not the machine. The seat. Keno's usually never free. Not without waiting in line a little while."

"Oh, I'm sorry. Were you waiting long?"

"Only every day, man."

"Okay."

"Know how to play keno? You don't look like you do."

I blush and laugh. "I thought I did. My mom taught me years ago, but it's been a bit."

"May I?"

"Please."

He leans over, hits a few of the white plastic buttons, and nods. "There. Try these bets."

"Oh. Thanks. I'm Marion."

"Diego," he says, holding out his hand while taking a drag of a cigarette. "Good to meet you, kid."

I return his nod, and he turns his focus back to his screen. I light up a cigarette, but I inhale too hard and cough. A fleck of ash breaks away from the cherry and flies right into my eye. I rub it away as I try a slower drag.

Five dollars disappears from my hand into the machine as I use the touch screen to shuffle through patterns of the blue numbers on the game cards, choose one that looks as good as any, and watch as the red circles appear. In eight bets, none of my chosen numbers are picked, and then I'm down to zero credits.

I yawn and throw in one last dollar. I see the credits screen change from zero to twenty, but it fades as I feel my eyes close. My head bobs down and pulls me back awake, and I fade in and out, from black to the bright keno neon.

From above, a new song plays on the speakers. A grating whistle over a marching beat. It startles me awake.

Before I can add to the amount of cash I wasted today, I see a dark shape in the corner of my right eye. I turn away from the flashing screen and see the old man from the gift shop at an intersection of banks.

"Hey, son, could you give me a hand?" he says, holding an empty Styrofoam cup.

A soft hand raps at my shoulder. I take a heavy breath as my head jerks upward, the slot machine reels a blur in front of me.

"Gotta stay awake, brother," Diego says. "The squadron has keen eyes to make sure you don't close yours."

I try to respond, but I only deliver a weak mumble. In the corner of the screen, the credits fade in and out under my lids.

The next time my eyes open, I pull myself away from the blue numbers and stand up. When I turn away from the machine, he's in the walkway again.

The casino is filled with old people. Most are friendly, but a gambling problem can turn a chipper person into a bitter mess quickly. I see none of that in this old man's smile. He looks like any white Minnesota grandfather, with a plaid coat and dark fishing hat.

But I didn't grow up with a grandfather. Nothing about this person feels familiar.

Before he can get closer, I grab my drink and leave in the opposite direction. The dollar I put in goes to waste, but it's a small price to pay to avoid talking to a stranger in my current state.

At the soda fountain, I finally get a chance to light a cigarette and refill. One step away, and it seems the old man is still following me. For a moment, I look into his eyes and wonder if this is some past lover of mine from down in the cities. Maybe he recognized me and is trying to approach me for another go. But I didn't recognize him through the glass window, and with every passing moment, he looks less familiar.

The ceiling speakers blare a muffled chorus over the same marching beat.

The casino floor is big enough that I should be able to lose this guy, but he's still there, smiling and walking with a cane.

He didn't have a cane before.

The cold metal of a slot bank hits my back. To my right he's closing in on me, his gait crooked and frail but with a determination to reach me.

He steps forward. I jump away and watch as he falls to the ground, his cane tumbling so close to me that it almost hits my ankle.

"Hey, bud, could you give an old guy a hand?"

There's that voice again, an unassuming, friendly voice with the touch of a Minnesota accent. But there's no hiding his eyes anymore. They're filled with an angry hunger, ugly gray irises around yellowing whites.

I hurry away as others notice the commotion. If I'd stayed any longer, they might've blamed me. But the patrons look away from the sight quickly and return to their screens. Back through the maze of banks, I'm somewhere near the edge of the casino floor, the front doors to my left.

The old man appears, blocking the beeline I could take to

leave. In each of his hands, a pair of wooden rhythm bones slide out of the gaps between his fingers.

I jog back the way I came and turn right after a few slot banks. Heat rushes to my face. The patrons around me whisper, and the security folk take notice. Instead of running down this aisle, where I assume he'll be waiting, I backpedal again and run for the doors.

I take one step just beyond the last row of machines, but as soon as my foot lands, I stop.

Something holds me in place.

He is at the end of the row, draped in shadows beyond where the winter sky's blue light is spilling in. I want to call out to someone, yell that this man is accosting me, but my jaw is locked. And who would listen?

All the patrons in this row are nodding, up and down, up and down—their faces pull back from hitting the game screen just in time, like a dreary fly-fishing cast.

The old man smiles and lifts his hands in front of him, one lower than the other. The playing bones twist from his fingers into his palms to form two crosses. He slowly alternates his hands up and down, as if he was holding puppet strings. They sway in time with the patrons.

"You have time for a few more spins, eh boy? Come. Sit and play."

I take a deep breath in and notice that my mouth has gone dry, and a rising tide of nausea washes over me. When I exhale, my nose and throat burn.

There's nothing on my arms, but it suddenly feels as if a litter of kittens are sinking their claws into my skin and pulling them upward.

My right leg almost buckles as I'm pulled forward. As my first step lands, my arms rise out in front of me. Invisible strings tighten around my forearms. My body is still slack as I take a few more steps, but through a strange, creeping numbness, I muster all the strength I can and yank my right arm back.

His hold breaks and leaves red-lined welts on my right arm, as if it had been wrapped with thick rubber bands. My left arm is still caught, and I feel him yank his same hand inward, now more forceful and angrier.

Just as I take another step, I feel a hand on my shoulder.

When I turn, there's a woman in a black suit with a radio in her hand. A Native girl, maybe not much older than me, her long hair held back in a bundle of braids, a pair of blue-shaded glasses above her small nose. As soon as I make eye contact, all the burning and nausea and claws on my arms dissipate.

At the end of the row, the old man is gone. I glance around me, and the patrons seem normal. Some still look rather sleepy, and a few look like they could nod off at any moment.

Her name tag says Alana. Close behind her is a casino security guard, another Native girl of similar age, but with clear glasses and a ponytail, staring at me. She's in a slate-gray, police-style uniform and has my coat draped over her arm, which sends my heart rate higher than it already was.

"Mr. Lafournier, would you mind coming with us?" Alana says. "We'd like to have a word with you."

Chapter 2   💀   SEVENFIRE SIGHT

CHERIE HALTSTORM

November 10, 2017

My nose has been through a lot over the years. And a lot has been through it. The thick, ghost-stale air of the casino's secondhand atmosphere, the mold in my parents' government house growing up, and my own stupidity sucked up through a straw. They all have done their damage.

Even so, I can still smell the weed pouring off this kid.

Alana and I lead him into a small office a few hallways down, empty except for a small table and four chairs. He drops into one and crosses nervous hands into his arms.

"Before we start," Alana says, grabbing the seat across from Marion. I drop my backpack in the seat next to her and stand a couple of feet back against the wall. "Do you trust me?"

The boy raises one of his heavy eyebrows and stutters, but after looking at Alana for a few moments, he nods shyly. Alana pulls out a small plastic bag filled with charcoal from inside her suit jacket. She grabs a small piece and then leans across the table and draws a few lines onto Marion's forehead. He sits still as a deer, blinking only once, slowly, when she pulls her hand back.

"What's that?" he asks.

"Just a little touch. Nothing untoward will bug you now." Alana smiles, straightens her shoulders, and resumes her professional affect. "I also want to assure you that there are no cameras or audio recording devices in this room."

Marion's face drains of color. "What? Why would—"

"We take our safety very seriously," I say. "But, eh, someone forgot to hook this room up, so it's one of the only private coves in this place."

"Am I in trouble?"

"From where you stood, you sure looked like it," Alana says. "You were acting very distressed. Like someone was chasing you."

"I—I don't know. There might've been someone. There was this . . ." The boy rubs his right temple and avoids eye contact. "Ya know, just an old man. I might've just fell asleep, and he startled me."

"A lot of our patrons aren't shy about beckoning the young'uns for a favor here or there. Maybe he was asking you for a coffee," I say.

"Or maybe he needed help to his car," Alana says.

"And you were just a little too high to understand the request."

His fidgeting hands retreat underneath his elbows, but he laughs. "Is it that obvious?" he says.

Alana keeps her professional smile up, but I laugh with him. "You're at the busiest casino on the rez, cuz. Not a soul in this trap doesn't know what weed smells like."

"Ya got me."

"It's quite all right," Alana says. "Of course, it might not be if we bring any canine officers around."

"But there's no need for that," I cut in. "Long as you're honest."

He takes a breath. "I mean, I guess for a bit, I had the passing thought that he was a ghost, or a spirit, maybe." His left eye twitches when he says the word *spirit*.

When I glance at Alana, she's smiling bigger now, and her eyes narrow behind those sky-colored glasses. She's needed them since we were teenagers. She started with a rosy-red pair, and they've darkened with each year. I'll need darker lenses one day, but I don't need them like she does yet.

"Not a spirit," she says. "But I think you might already sense that, cousin."

"Oh, are we cousins?"

"Aren't we?" I chide. "Small world, ya know."

"If you're my cousin," Alana says, "it would explain a few things about your aura. You have the eyes of a doubting Thomas, sure, but it seems like you recently helped a spirit pass on."

He throws his hands up. "S'pose it wouldn't do any good to deny it if it's that evident to you."

Alana taps at the corner of her glasses with a Hidden Atlantis–branded ballpoint pen. "Eyes like a Bullhead. On the night I had my first moon, I was allowed to learn about sevenfire sight."

The women in the family never told me any of the things Alana says they told her. Not our great aunt Elise, none of our aunts, not even a few of the older cousins with loose lips. Part of me never wanted to believe her because of that, but I guess I knew there was something. I don't know if that was just the luck of the draw that none of those sevenfire wisps are in my eyes. Or maybe I just never earned their trust.

Either I fucked it up myself, or it's all just old lady whispers. Alana's needed those prescription lenses forever, and she's always been more responsible than me, so it's not out of the question that her soul's a little older than mine and that she'd settle into believing the old wives' tales long before I do.

"So. Who was he?" Alana smiles, and the boy's shoulders finally relax.

"Long story, really. I have a bet, though, since it's a casino and on this rez and all. Bet you once I say the name, you'd know those long details already. Kayden Kelliher."

Now my own shoulders tense up, and even through her glasses, her shock is as obvious as mine.

Eight long seconds pass. All I can picture is my auntie Brenda's son Jared, razor-faced and in an orange jumpsuit.

"Time and a place," Alana says, clearing her throat, "for all things. Right now, my only concern is our patrons."

"Right," I say, kicking back into gear. "Ya know, we really got to make a good impression and give our guests the service they deserve."

"And apparitions, whatever they are, make bad business."

"So. What do you want from me then?" Marion asks.

Alana leans in. "Remember what we said. There's no microphones in this room. You aren't the first one who's seen him. Our cameras have not. You won't find him anywhere in the data."

"I don't believe in much," I chime in. "But there was one night, when I was sneaking a nap in an old storage room. I could've sworn I found someone's handwriting on a spool of nickel paper. Had to be a dude's writing, all that ugly scratch . . . it talked about something he called a sandman in the shadows of the lower hallways. When I woke up, I remembered where I was. Back of the bank rolling coin for the money stations. Never found a trace of the writing on those nickel rolls." I sigh and feel a cold spasm through my neck. "There's at least one other crazy person out there who might've seen some old stalker running about."

Marion twiddles at his fingernails. "Not even six months ago, I woulda told you I didn't believe in anything supernatural. I don't even know if Kayden was a good spirit, but eventually, when he did leave, it wasn't a bad feeling. Peaceful. This thing on the casino floor was all the opposite. Nothing but sickness. Bad medicine."

"You know about bad medicine?" Alana muses.

"Not really, but I know the way Indians' voices drop when they talk about it."

"Bad medicine is bad for the casino business," Alana says. "I do remember you, I think. Weren't you talking about ghosts in middle school?"

He chuckles. "Not that I recall."

"If it wasn't you, then it was another boy who didn't know a ghost from a sheet. But I do know ghosts. Trust me, Marion. Sometimes they hitch a ride in our bingo vans. Can be a real scare to a few of our passengers, but a sighting now and then pushes interest more than it pushes people out the door. But that's not the case lately. There's a lot more ghosts on the route to Indian Hollow. Have you ever heard the stories about Indian Hollow?"

He shakes his head.

"They say eagles don't fly there. Not even a pow-wow will bring them. And no matter if you're coming or going, ghosts will hitch a ride with you."

"Huh. I did hear of that part. Ghosts like to hitch a ride."

Alana's voice drops. "That's what I'm counting on. I need you to lead them away from the casino. Toward Indian Hollow. And help them pass on."

"Why me?"

Alana's shoulders straighten up. She's in her professional casino host voice. "This is a place of *business*, Mr. Lafournier. Our upper-management types, they're not really concerned with anything but running a tight ship. Making sure the customers have a good time and the employees are staying in line and doing their best." She drops the white-lady affect, her voice now almost a whisper. "They don't deal with anything of this sort."

"Think about the paperwork, sparky," I cut in. "No manager wants to deal with an employee's superstitions or a customer who thinks he may have seen something. So in not so many words, they ask peons like us if we can look into it."

"And we do, but sometimes we're stretched too thin. Sometimes we're short staffed. I'd trust a cousin who barely knows us—no offense—over anyone else."

Marion sighs. "I can't exactly promise I can help them pass on. Or that they'll follow me."

I shrug. "Nothing wrong with giving it the ol' college try." I walk forward and dig into my backpack. "Ya know, I don't think I remember seeing you at Uncle Froglegs's funeral."

Even without looking at her, I can feel Alana glare at me, and Marion blushes and sputters.

"I—I'm sorry. I don't—it's just—my mom's usually the one who tells me about these things."

"I didn't see her there either," Alana says. "That's not really like Hazel, is it?"

Marion shakes his head. "No. She's always there to help."

"Exactly. Lot of odd things happening on this rez lately."

I pull out a black jacket from the bag. Worn and patchy from years of wear. Dark, curly specks hang off of the fabric like aspen leaves in a breeze. Each sleeve has a checkerboard flag pattern on the bicep, and the front is white with two big horizontal stripes. "This belonged to him. And I got stuck with giving that old froggy bastard's clothes to friends and family."

I set the coat on the table in front of Marion. His gaze and frame both freeze in shock.

"Our family looks out for each other," Alana says. "I promise you that."

The boy stares at the jacket for ten long seconds. He blinks, nods weakly, and scoops the jacket into his arms. "I knew something would keep me here," he mumbles.

When he walks out of the office, Alana and I exchange silent glances, each of us wondering, too late, if this is a good idea.

Chapter 3 ♣ MEDICINE REEL

MARION LAFOURNIER

November 10, 2017

"How long do you need me to stall? Your auntie is expecting you in a few hours."

"I really don't know, Mom."

"Any estimate at all?"

"Can't rightly say. Do you remember last summer? When the . . . ?"

"Yes."

"It's kind of like that. Again."

Earlier in the year, I accidentally brought a dog spirit back to life. He played as cheerfully as any lonely pup, but beneath there was something else in that thing that I never got an answer about. Something that felt more vicious and primal. I've been hoping it was just the feral part of the creature from when it was alive. My mom, Hazel, was sure it wasn't just a normal dog but a half-wolf hybrid, and it followed me hours away to her place. Before last summer, I think I had seen only one of these oft-talked-about beasts of the rez.

Hazel disappeared for nearly a week, chasing that thing through the woods and, from her telling, to some world beyond.

To her, it felt like no more than an hour she'd been gone, but my stepdad Anni insisted later that she was gone a week. Neither of us could get a hold of her by phone. So before I even attempt to do this thing for Alana and Cherie, when I'm not even sure if I can do it, I let my mother know I could be gone a while.

"I'll take care of things for you, kiddo. Just stay safe."

"I'll try."

"*Gigawaabamin.*" I'll see you again.

"You too. Promise."

I hang up, walk out of the casino, and pocket the phone. There's another man on his phone standing about ten yards away from me under the casino atrium. He wears a light maroon jacket over a pastel-yellow golf shirt, puffy gray cargo shorts with a flamingo pattern that flap loosely in the early winter wind, and shin-high black socks above tan flip-flops.

If the November cold bothers him, his loudly confident voice doesn't show it. His frame doesn't keep still. He shifts on his ankles often and rolls his shoulders back and forth, one hand in his pocket, the other holding a slate-gray phone to his ear.

At first, I feel compelled to walk away, so that he's not under the impression that I was eavesdropping, but his light clothing for this time of year gives me pause and then halts me in place. Normally, it wouldn't faze me, growing up in the North where the pride of handling the weather is often competitive. There's nothing too out of the ordinary about some guy who isn't bundled up in winter, on or off reservation.

But that's the thing. The normalcy, the innocuous picture in front of me. Could it be another cover? That presence in the casino, with his veneer of commonality, nearly took me unaware.

The man in the cargo shorts turns his head to me, and after three long seconds of eye contact, he winks, and the grin on his boisterous face grows wider.

"All right, looking forward to catching up later, old friend," he says. He ends the call and turns fully in my direction. "Beautiful day we're having." He takes a deep breath of the crisp air. "Nice and warm."

There's that cold weather pride again. As I stand wrapped in my thick gray overcoat and scarf, with not a trace of skin showing below the waist, the line feels like both a taunt and a flirtation.

"Not cold?"

"Not at all. Minnesota skin." He thumps his fist on his chest twice, and the gaudy yellow of the golf shirt keeps my gaze there when he says, "Maybe you need some of it on you."

I can't help but laugh. "I'm fine with a coat and a thermos." I hold up the empty casino thermos. "Keeps me plenty warm."

The man pulls out a green cigarette box from his flamingo shorts and uses a metal Minnesota Vikings lighter. "Name's Glenn. From around here, bud?" He holds out the menthol pack to me, but I shake my head and decline.

"Not lately."

"What's that mean?"

"That I was just leaving," I say, and finally, I feel my foot taking a step away from him.

"What's the rush?"

"Just anxious to get moved in."

Before I can take another step, the casino door opens. It's Cherie.

"Mr. Nielan?" she says. "It'll be a bit longer before our host can meet you."

"No problem, ma'am."

"Can we bring you anything? A coffee or a soft drink?"

"Oh, I'm just fine out here, but thank you."

Cherie glances at me. "Hey. Good luck, cousin," she says, and as quickly as she appeared, she ducks back inside, the door lingering in the last few inches with a mechanical whir.

"So what were we saying? Something about your name and number?" He takes a few steps toward me until he's within arm's reach, and he focuses that sparkle of interest in his eyes directly on me.

But with Cherie's interruption comes a respite from my building suspicion and fear. Glenn seems to be just an ordinary, if forward, human. Not Alana's sandman. With him this close, I notice his wide shoulders and the tightness of his golf shirt over his muscled chest. His face is handsome, if a bit tired, and his short hair, a mix of copper brown and silver, is receding just enough to look charming. Were it an ordinary day, I might've been more receptive to his growing interest, but I want to get away from this place as quickly as possible.

"Gavin," I say. "And I don't have a number. Gave up my phone for Lent."

"Lent is over."

"Yeah, but I was just saving so much money I never renewed."

"But you said you're moving? Sounds dangerous, a boy on the road all alone."

"I'll manage."

"Your pocket is giving your lie away, Gav," he says, head nodding toward my leg.

I shrug and laugh. "Guess lying to dudes just comes easy to me."

"Where did you say you were moving to?"

"I didn't." I point off in the distance toward the tree line south of the building. "But that way, more or less."

"What's the reason for your move? I've been considering relocating here myself."

I smile and then bridge the gap between us by half, so his frame is now a few inches from mine. "To get away from the men up here. They're a bit too old to keep up with me."

"Boy, you are just asking for me to bring you up to my room and break your misconceptions."

"Just too bored up here." I shrug. "There was also an ex of mine. Wanted a little distance from him." I take a step back, and he follows.

"Well, you know the quickest way to get over a guy . . ."

"Go on a solo spiritual journey, eh?" I clap him on the shoulder as if he were a normal friend, hoping to finally dissuade him. But also, a bit of a test. His arm is normal, tangible. Not the blurry nightmare that old man inside devolved into.

He cocks his head and his eyes narrow. "Do you like dogs?"

"Yeah. Had one until recently. Actually, I left him with that ex I mentioned."

"Oh, is that so? I've had to do that with an ex or two. You miss him?"

"Sure. But I figure maybe it's for the best anyway. More space up here, and honestly, everyone thought I was a bad trainer."

Glenn lights another cigarette. "I'm a good pup trainer." He exhales, and a smoke cloud fills the space between us. "At least, I thought I was. I had a falling out with a few pups not too long ago. They moved out and blocked my number. And I was really getting attached to them."

I laugh. "Oh. Did you think I meant a guy? A puppy-suited guy?"

"You didn't?"

I purse my lips and shake my head. "Not even in the slightest. An actual dog. A rez dog, with fur. And shoe-chewing abilities."

"You don't think a boy like you could learn how to chew shoes?"

"Oh, Jesus Christ . . ." is all I can say as I shake my head and blush.

"Like I said, I'm a very good trainer."

Just then, a casino shuttle bus pulls into the atrium, and a group of older couples cautiously steps out onto the slightly icy pavement. Glenn backs away a step or two and throws his hands in his pockets, shoulders tensed as the new guests arrive, but his gaze stays strong on mine.

I take the moment to finally take a few steps away. "Good luck, Glenn. Hope you win big."

I can see he wants to follow, or to say something back, but the presence of other people seems to dampen the confidence he'd worn. It's only when the bus pulls away and all the customers are inside that his focus returns to me.

"Come play a few spins with me. I've got a little cash to spend." He winks. "All I ask is half of whatever you win." I see his eyes dart down to my lips and then up to my forehead. "What's this?"

I grab his wrist before he can touch my face. He stops, but I can tell by the touch of his arm he could easily overwhelm my own if he meant to. "None of your business," I say softly. "But okay. I'll spend your money if you want me to." He stifles what sounded like the start of a giggle and pulls me back toward the casino by the hand.

Cherie gives us a beaming customer service smile as we walk past. Glenn leans against me and says, "Pick your favorite slot machine," into my ear with breath that reeks of cigarettes—though to be fair, it's no worse than the rest of the atmosphere in here.

I shake my head and laugh. "Any's fine. Doesn't matter to me."

He drags me to a tall machine with a curved screen that hovers above us both, displaying a stack of neon-yellow dollar amounts. The game is called *Big Beedle Bucks!* From his pocket, he produces one hundred dollars in twenties and puts it in my hand. "Go wild."

I blush. I'm not really used to being handed cash by men in public places. I look up. "Shouldn't you, like. Not?"

"Relax, *Gavin*." He digs his hands into my shoulders until I sit in the chair and feed another twenty down the gullet. "They know me here. We'll be fine."

Once again, I find myself staring at a matrix of betting lines I don't understand flashing over tiles of illustrated miscellanea that I also don't understand, and a few times I win some credits. Glenn sets it to five dollars a spin. When the first hundred is gone, after a couple dozen spins or so, he hands me another to throw in. His right arm rests on my left shoulder, while his other hand gestures over the screen as I spin. He gives some explanation about what the lines mean, all through a stiff voice as the edge of his mouth held in a freshly lit cig.

"So what's your real name, sir?"

"Can't it just stay Gavin?"

"Even after two hundred bucks for you? Got some nerve, bud."

When I turn to him, I think he's waiting for the kiss. I turn back to the screen right as a new spin yields 355 credits. "Marion."

"Heh. How about a last name? Ya know I come from around here too. I might just know your folks."

"Nah, ya don't. I'm sure."

Behind us, a server wheels by, offering refreshments. Glenn grabs a paper basket with two skewers of tropical fruit. "Hungry?"

"Not really."

"More for me."

Glenn slurps down the fruit, and in front of me, a row of cherries nets me three thousand more credits.

"Each credit is a penny, right?"

"Yep."

"So I just won thirty-five fifty on one spin?"

"*We* just won," he says with a wink.

A flood of gold coins falls across Glenn's screen. By the time a worker helps him claim it, the final number is $535. "Not bad," he says. Then he smiles and drops his voice even lower. "Would you like to come up to my hotel room? Maybe we play a little more there and then come back, put in a little more work here."

However long I must have considered his offer was probably just a few seconds too long because I could see the hope in his eyes just before I shook my head. "Nah. Nah, I should get going. I'm sorry."

I leave him to his spins and hurry back outside. He wasn't an unattractive man by any means, and where better to indulge a little hedonism than a place like this? There are worse noons than spending a few hundred of a handsome man's dollars, even one wearing a golf polo and sandals.

Back in the skunky interior of my hot-boxed sedan, I put on the race car jacket Cherie gave me, and then I pull the car out of the parking lot as quick as I can, disturbing the same flock of french-fry-eating white pigeons as when I came in. The sky is cloudier than it was this morning, and a light snow is falling, disappearing into the slick tar but slowly accumulating on the pale grass on the roadsides. Behind the casino, Jackson Lane runs ten miles or so to Indian Hollow, the road where Alana says the problem is.

On the right is a small road leading to a cemetery, where the casino is still visible through a copse of dead, thin shrubbery. I park my car a few yards in the road and let it idle while I catch my bearings.

In the mirror, I notice the lines of charcoal are still on my forehead. I rub at the beginnings, or perhaps the last remains, of a migraine just above my eyes. Ah. That grating roar of the slot machines. That air, stale and thick like an old newspaper lining a break room ashtray. I don't really remember why I went back into the casino, but my sore temples remember it well enough.

I light the second of the six joints to help me think about ghosts. Where to start in this fool's errand my Bullhead cousins have sent me on. Google seems like the most obvious place.

Opening up my phone, I type in the search bar "exorcism" but then delete it. That term seems way too violent and combative to these ghosts, so I instead type "respectful exorcism how to."

The first result is about clandestine Catholic exorcisms all across Minnesota. I avoid that one. If that's true, I don't need it in my browser history. Last time I was in a church, a ghost boy talked to me, and luckily it was my friend Gerly and not some buff exorcist from the diocese who overheard me. Best not to take this matter to the church.

The next two pages are filled with fun facts about exorcisms, their methods and misconceptions, salt and water, and a few odd articles exploring whether the ritual should make a comeback.

I glance over to the plastic casino bag with the variety herbs inside and decide to plug that in the search bar next. After "sage g" the first suggestion is "sage ghost removal." The first page is filled with many paranormal blogs and how-tos, and a few of them don't even load right. The shoddy service in this neck of the woods and the barrage of ads that pop up reset the website to the top over and over.

I sigh and lock the phone screen. Near the end of the joint, my car and mind are about the same level of foggy, and there's a shadowed figure in the back seat.

"DIY ghost hunting?" the voice says. Male. Older. Native.

"Pretty much," I reply. "Be lying if I said I didn't feel way out of my depth."

"Then why accept the girls' challenge? Yeah, let's call it a challenge."

I tilt my head back and take the last hit of the disappearing joint number two. "I don't know. I did that thing I do. Agree to whatever asked when I'm high and regret it later."

"You seem pretty unprepared for all they ask of you, boy."

I turn around to face the specter, but he's obscured by the smoke. "I always am. Still, gotta help the family, nah?"

Through the dissipating haze I see a smile grow on his face.

"A lesson I learned way too late in life, boy."

"It's Marion."

"It's 'Nameless Boy,' far as I'm concerned. You look like you're missing something. Not all there to my spirit's eyes, *niiji*."

"Are you the one Cherie called Old Froglegs?"

"Bet you don't know my real name."

"You'd win." I shrug. "Auntie Gwen showed me the

extended family tree a few times, but there's so many to keep track of."

"Best keep it to Ol' Froglegs then."

"Okay, Ol' Froglegs. So why are you here? Have they found the kids that did that to you?"

"Nah. They might, someday. Full confidence in our red boys in blue over at the tribal police department. I'm not concerned about that. They were just kids. Maybe a lifetime of guilt in or out of jail will heal them someday."

"What are your concerns, Froglegs?"

"Concerned as shit that Alana asked for help from someone in the family who keeps his drugs in a candy box in his front seat."

"Hey, the family taught me this method at pretty much every funeral."

"You should've hung out with me more, nephew. I'da taught you how an adult handles his stash."

I put the car in reverse and pull back out onto Jackson Lane. "I guess we have some time now." My ghostly great-uncle smiles, and his wispy form drifts forward to the passenger seat.

Six miles east of Waubajeeg, Jackson Lane turns into County Road 35, with a nauseating speed limit of only fifty miles per hour. The first few miles are through winding woods, and at this rate it'll take almost forty-five minutes to reach Indian Hollow.

I've been on this route only once or twice, when my mother was younger and we took a trip to swim at Little Swede Beach.

I crack the windows and the sunroof to air out the car. After an awkward silence between me and the translucent man next to me, I try to make conservation.

"Real shame I didn't meet you while you were alive."

"Why didn't you?"

I shrug. "Just wasn't around."

"I've heard that before from young folk. Even my own son."

"It's true, though. I lived a few miles out of town. Didn't really like going anywhere with my mom. What's your son's name?"

"Edenfield Junior. Used to go by EJ when he still liked me. He isn't around much either."

There was regret in his voice. My luck must've turned around, considering that the first spirit I need to help pass on is a family member with sonny issues.

"How old is he?"

"Almost thirty now. Works construction down in the cities."

"Were you estranged?"

"For most of his life, but after I lost my second leg, he came back around and let me meet the grandkids."

At the mention of his legs, I glance down at the passenger side floor. "Looks like you got them back, though. Can you feel them?"

He bellows out another booming laugh. "I don't know if I'm feeling anything but amusement at your naivete, Marion. Sure nice to see them there." A silver tear flows down his face. "Anything I feel blows away easy as wind."

"I see. So how did your name become Froglegs?"

He falls silent for a long time. Nearly a full minute passes before he bows his head and lets out what sounds like a deep exhale. "I've been gambling since I was a toddler, son." The strain in his voice thickens the air. I turn on the heat and light the third joint from the Altoids can.

"Wanna hit?"

Ol' Froglegs takes the joint from my fingertips. "You don't even know what a hit is, boy." It's odd watching his already smoky form fill up with smoke, like a party trick involving a condom and a bong.

"My first gamble was believing that the Bellerose kids were really gonna give me vodka if I jumped off Quarry Way bridge. I knew their father was a blind pig, ya know. Just like your great-grandfather was, up through Canada. He didn't do that after Bullhead died, though."

I can't tell if it's the weed that's making him ramble and spill or if it's just what his restless soul needs, but his voice does seem calmer, airier. I'm hoping he's closer to wherever he needs to go.

"I jumped off that damn bridge, and my older cousins had to rescue me. They laughed at how I kicked in the water when I was in a full panic. So there ya go. I became Froggy Legs. Looks like it changed with age."

He hands me the joint, and on the first draw to my lips, it seems a little colder, like his propinquity added some menthol flavor. As I exhale a big hit, I see those silvery tears again, not just on his cheeks but the whole shape, his eyes shimmery pools like burnished nickels.

"They were so cruel to a little boy," Froglegs says. "I understand now, but then I didn't. They saw the boy had the sevenfire sight, but it was growing too fast too early. They made him stop. Said they'd teach me when I was old enough, but that never came. And what sight he could use, well . . . it didn't work like it does for the girls. Woulda been nice to know how to avoid losing my legs."

I take another big hit from the joint. It's all guesswork, of course, but it feels like he's closer to moving on.

He lets out a pained howl, low and gravelly at first but

fluttering to a higher shriek. His arm jerks forward, a curled finger swatting at the passenger-side dashboard, as if he were trying to mash a button, but convulsive, verging on epileptic.

"I miss my machines so much. That's what the memory of the sight feels like, boy. The good fortune that you can see ahead of you so clear. It feels like that every time you walk into a casino. Have you felt that before? When you walk into that maze of lights and you think, *This time for sure*, because it didn't happen last time, but . . . but you know it's coming. Do you know that feeling, Marion?"

"Like I said, I don't really gamble."

I pause and think about when I first arrived at Hidden Atlantis. I never planned on spending any excess time there. I only wanted to drain the snake, get back on the road, and find busier bustling adventures down in the gray, labyrinthine dregs of the Twin Cities. But instead, I bought more cigarettes, even though I haven't been a habitual nicotine user for a few months. I bought a pack of those ridiculous variety herbs even though I seldom get involved in the spiritual tangles in the culture, and I lost nearly fifty dollars on machines I hadn't used in about eight years.

"Hey, uncle. Do you think this sandman could be pulling people into Atlantis somehow?"

His translucent face considered this, a slow smile spreading across it. "The fear in Cherie's and Alana's voices and eyes tell me this foul being is some evil from beyond. No telling what kind of bad medicines he controls. You know that one swampy flower? It looks like a little purple test tube. It brings in flies with a body full of stinky nectar. Not out of the question to think your sandman can do that."

I pause.

"My sandman?"

As Froglegs speaks, I notice the first passenger in the rear-view mirror.

"Oh, here they come." Froglegs pats his wrist, once bare but now covered in dozens, maybe well over a hundred wristwatches. "Like clockwork."

The ghosts go dancing one by one, hurrah, hurrah

The slot machines have won by one, hurrah, hurrah

Chapter 4 ☠ THE CLOCKWORK GHOSTS

November 10, 2017

The first ghost is an older woman with a black wool coat over a cashmere sweater, long silver curls that fall just past her ears, and big, round glasses with thick, coffee-colored lenses. Unlike Froglegs, she's not ethereal; she looks like a normal old lady who just happened to sneak into my car.

The woman is staring out the window.

I hold up a hand to Froglegs and glance back for a moment. "Hello?"

"Oh, I just don't know if we have time to get to the casino before the drawing," she says.

"We're heading away from the casino right now."

"I'll never hear the end of it from my daughter." The ghost sighs. "I promised her I wouldn't be late for once."

I look to Froglegs for help, but he shrugs with a tight-lipped smile.

"Is your daughter waiting for you, miss?"

She finally turns away from the window and makes eye contact with me through the mirror. "Aren't you a little young to be a bingo driver?"

When I look at my face in the mirror, I see the face that used to greet me in the mornings before getting ready for middle school. My breath gets caught in my throat; Froglegs reaches over and holds the steering wheel steady.

"I don't think she can see beyond her time."

I relax my breath and start to ask her when she died but stop myself and rethink the question. "What's the occasion for the drawing?"

"Oh, just the usual New Year's Eve prize."

"How much is the pot?"

"Two thousand two dollars. I hate to put our hopes on it, but lordy could we use that cash."

I feel a lump in my throat again. I open one of my energy drinks just to wash it down and calm myself. She must have died when I was only ten years old.

"What's your name, ma'am?"

"Jeanine. Jeanine Gentle."

"It's nice to meet you, Jeanine." I can feel my fingers trembling on the wheel. "I have to apologize, though. I'm not going to the casino right now. But is there someplace else I can bring you?"

Jeanine sighs and rests her small fist against her cheek. "Maybe it's best I miss the drawing. I shouldn't rely on gambling or my daughter to pay my bills." She looks at me again. "Where are you going, hun?"

"Right now, I think I'm going to Indian Hollow."

Her eyes swell to big white discs. The irises fade to a dull, flowery gray. "No, no." Her arms glower from a tangible form to wispy flashes as she pats at her coat pockets, muttering about a purse that isn't there. "My daughter's paycheck. All of it. It was in there . . ."

Quick as she appeared she's gone, and as soon as the back seat is empty, I let out a big breath and take in several smaller ones. After a few seconds, I'm able to draw in through the nose slowly again.

"What the hell was that?" I say as I rub a sudden headache on the center of my forehead.

"Spirits walk a lonely winter. It's not such a good time, is it?"

I shake my head so hard my glasses jiggle. "No."

"Careful what you sign up for, little cousin."

Before I can stop him, Froglegs grabs another joint from the tin.

"It's rude to smoke with passengers in the car, don'tcha know?" says a man's voice.

Two new passengers are in the back seat: a middle-aged man and woman, him in a boxy, faded suit, and her in a floral blouse with layers of metal jewelry on her wrists and neck.

"Sorry. I'm new to driver's etiquette." I hold back a dry cough as my uncle fumigates the car. "Would you care to join, though?"

"Oh, could we?" the woman says, her voice full of exasperation and impatience. "This has been such a vacation from hell."

"Oh, here we go!" the man says. "Ya knows the cabins and the casino were *your* idea. I'm trying to have fun, but you keep fighting me on everything!"

A twinge of cold pain erupts at the tip of my finger as the ghostly hand grabs the joint from mine. The woman reaches in her bra, and her eyes glower with the same blaze-white discs as the older woman. Even though I can't see her irises in the rearview mirror anymore, I recognize that panic is sending her into these jagged convulsions. "Honey, please tell me you have the jackpot money."

The steering wheel shakes loosely under my fingers, which are chilled from tips to wrist.

"Which site are we going to?" Another ghost appears, this time sitting between the convulsing married couple. A young Native man with a bear claw and feather tatted around his left eye. "I'm tryna get to Magic Midnight in Kildere."

A fourth ghost appears, now sitting on the husband's lap, but the pair is reduced to scratchy lines as the fifth came in. A sixth, a seventh, eighth, ninth, cramming wherever they could go.

"Hey, could you stop at a gas station? I need some smokes."

"Could you spot me for a pack when you get them? I can't find my wallet," says another.

"Mine's gone too!"

An ugly chorus of voices, half shouting different places on the reservation they wish to be and half lamenting about their misplaced cash. The spinning white discs in their eyes splash a crimson red, not the hue of a man's veins, but the spotty matte of fading paint. Their forms fill the car as easily as they smoke, but as they leave there is nothing in their wake but a pulsing hurricane of black, white, and red lights. I take my foot off the gas, and when I try to breathe again, there's no movement of air.

*

"Uncle."

The wheel is shaking in my hands, and the tip of my tongue is burned raw as more smoke passes over.

"Uncle, stop. The money. We have to find the money."

"Smoke up, neph. We never got to smoke together when I was alive, member?"

*

Half a line of cocaine, half a mind to null the dull pain

Familiar words like an old friend, spinning over and over in my head like a merry-go-round, but how could they be mine? That was never my drug of choice, but there it is, piled in a neat line in front of me on the poker table.

But when I look around, I don't see the casino. All I see is a simple garage-like den. A cheap garage, too—one of those cheap townhouses on the north side of the city, made to look like a man's den, complete with two old and worn poker tables, each filled with rows of red coins. The line goes up my nose.

I've been here before, this strange, cold nowhere land. When Kayden's spirit borrowed my body. I saw the life he dreamed of as a child, all that grief as it faded away from him. *I came back from that*, I repeat to myself. *I came back.*

Through this man's eyes, I see a handful of ghosts surround his poker table setup. They goad him about his poker-playing prowess, and in his frenzied state, he takes his truck fifteen miles down the road to the great golden hall of Atlantis.

The last thing I see is a pool of brown across the velveteen carpet, the collection from the wad of menthol snuff tucked below my teeth, as the casino security guards surround my convulsing body. The guard readies a syringe of Narcan for my limp arm.

Chasing fentanyl across the land has never been so easy!

Because he'd landed on his side, his final thought was the realization that somewhere out on the casino floor, he'd dropped his wallet.

I feel my vision pull away from the collapsed man's body. Below, I can see the clockwork ghosts. They wander in jagged circles across the casino floor. The man with the poker tables and tobacco spit. A boy with moon-black eyes, screaming at the slot machine in agony before dropping, hands clawing at his chest. Two young women on a cheap motel bed, their bodies alternating between heaving and being angelic and still, the sheets bespeckled with black and brown, like bites and kisses from hungry, powder-silk moths. A man without legs in a wheelchair, another man without legs without a wheelchair, and an older woman with a silky, white robe, helping the men make their way through the maze. Hundreds of voices in agonized laughter, echoing from underneath the keno section.

One of the ghostly forms, not the one that was just in my head but one of the ghosts he saw in his life, is seated at his poker table. Lonnie Barclay.

I knew him. Or I knew of him.

The memory sends a pulse through me, anchoring me back to the casino floor.

Earlier this year my friend Gerly told me what she knew about her boyfriend Kayden's death. Jared Haltstorm blamed Kayden when Lonnie died in a meth lab explosion. It's this memory, this reminder of life, of reality and of this ugly reservation, that brings me back.

*

I look over at Froglegs. There's color in his eyes now, two spinning irises like a leathery net with purple and pale green shades throughout, speckled with drops of white glass.

His hands rip open the plastic bag of sacred herbs. He raises the bundle of sage to his mouth, and the remnants of his teeth crunch down, black-and-purple smoke rising from the crunching strands.

Outside the slowing car, the wheels tumble over the shoulder into tall grass. My arms lie slack at my side, and my head bobs back forth.

"How much music you got churning in your skull now?" the man next to me says.

"You're . . . not Froglegs." The *F* in his name falls off of my tongue and hangs half over my bottom lip, drooling.

His skin, once misty and translucent, has swirled into a writhing but solid mass, and a thousand lines of wrinkles and chins fill the rest of his face.

"What do the two thick bars and the two black balls mean?"

"You're the *maji-manidoo* . . ."

"Incorrect. *Manidookaazo.* You can play pretend, can't you, boy?"

A voice not my own takes control of my tongue, though it still lolls. *"Repeat. Repeat! Repeat!"*

Even this far away, I can sense a cold void where the words came from. The voice of a ghost under the slot banks, screaming from the unmoving mouth of a quarter painted red. His frail voice reaches through me like a lifeline.

"Very good." The sandman's fingers stroke the hair above my right ear and then trail down the scruff on my chin and neck. "How about the one that looks like a sacred medicine wheel? Oh, don't be shy now. You know you've seen it around. On silk-screened posters, maybe a promotional pen? Oh, they opted for gel ink. That's the good stuff. C'mon, lad. Name that medicine wheel."

I try to reply, but my eyes are as heavy as my arms.

"Hey, quick thought. What if the medicine wheel, much like in a well-written musical masterpiece, is the last thing you see before you stop? When that final reel spins the wheel and you need the crescendo to crash and then the silence, what if that's what you see?"

The car thumps and shakes as it drifts toward the left side of the highway. In the distance I can see a bridge.

With one last attempt, I bring my heavy arms up. My left hand manages to grab the wheel, and my right misses but lands on the column-shift behind. The sandman puts his lips near the bottom of my ear, the air of his breath scratching across my neck like black exhaust.

"It's called a coda."

Chapter 5 ☠ CAME ROLLING HOME

MARION LAFOURNIER

November 10, 2017

In my hand, the crank. Not a column shift.

I pull it down, the metal gears clanking like a smoothly bridged deck of cards. It floats back upright, and on-screen blue circles scatter across the game-card of red numbers. Eight of mine are chosen. The coin hopper bursts open, and there's a rain of nickels at my feet. The screen lights up, and the bonus music plays.

Da-da-da da-da daaa daa.

The machine is called *King Maker Keno.*

"Cups, my man! Cups!"

Diego places a large plastic cup with the Hidden Atlantis logo on the side underneath the hopper spout. Many coins are already scattered around my feet.

There are cheers around me, and suddenly there are several casino employees standing nearby, watching, laughing, congratulating. One of the guards gathers up the scattered nickels while a machine worker opens the slot door and tinkers with a big bag and box of coins, bills, and tickets. Eventually, the employees take the three cups of nickels, some kind of library rental card paperwork, and my driver's license.

"Lucky you," Diego says as the attendant brings me eleven hundred dollars in crisp, blue bills. "First time playing, first jackpot, and no taxes. Beginner's luck." He winks. "Believe it."

I stare at the money in my hand.

Diego nudges me, leans in, and whispers, "They're waiting for a tip, young gun."

"Oh! Right. I, uh . . ."

Before I stammer out of control, I hand the employee a fifty-dollar bill. He thanks me and walks away.

It feels as if there are several conversations all around me—the guy who helped with the nickel cups, the guards, the other patrons—and even though I can't hear myself talk inside or out, I have the distinct feeling that I've been speaking.

"Got any for me, cuz? I did show you how to play. Neh."

I look at the stack of bills. They're so pale, like a glass of milk that's curdled and now has lined patterns of green mold over it. They wilt in my grip like crumpled wrapping paper. Series 1985 next to a swooping *J* name. Johnny, maybe.

I hand the entire stack over to Diego, to his surprise.

"Hoh, I don't know about that, bud. They got eyes in the sky, ya know. Imagine how it looks from afar."

I glance around the casino, up and down, from the bright golden ceiling of gods, all interspersed with navy-blue plastic bulbs whose sea-murky tint hides the tiny cameras behind. It's a nice mural, but the scattering of plastic domes makes it look like some of the figures have giant blue welts or growths on their otherwise Adonis bodies.

Or maybe they are arranged to look like the zodiac. An array of the constellations made of dozens of panopticons. And instead of a star map it just looks like a pox.

Beyond the slot bank I sit at, all the others are bright and blurry because few of them have lights that are not in a constant flurry.

Da-da-da da-da daaa daa.

"Please keep it," I say. "I have to go."

I beeline my way to the bar and sit, not daring to look around me again.

"Beer," I say. "Whatever you got."

The bartender fills a glass from a tap with a dark green eelpout on the label. "EelPA, courtesy of Indian Hollow Brewing Company."

"Great."

"We're also doing two-for-one pull tabs this week."

"How much are they?"

"Two dollars."

"Okay."

I put down a twenty-dollar bill, and the bartender drops a big handful of cardboard circles. The back design is that of a generic poker chip, with the three tabs in front hiding either riches or money loss.

Slowly, all sixty tabs tear, and none of the fruit or bars or 7s on the other side align with fortune, but the sound of the paper ripping is calming.

"Alana or Cherie working today?"

"Who?" he says while swabbing the black oak counter with a hunter's-orange microfiber tea towel.

"One's a security guard." I pause, reinspecting each of the pull tabs in case I missed a pattern. "I don't really know what Alana is but she had a pantsuit."

"Been here a while, sir. I don't recognize either of those names. There's a Laura, but she doesn't really work security, per se."

"What's that mean?"

"Well, the county did her police training and helps us with drug bustin', but we don't sign her paychecks. She's around, though."

"Mm. Okay."

I put down a ten-dollar bill and open another set of ten.

This time my luck takes an easy turn. Three two-dollar winners.

I collect the money, leave half for a tip, and then make for the door.

At the front entrance, the lanky blond security guard, Zach, who Alana had referred to as her baby daddy, is holding a drunk-looking *me* firmly on the right shoulder and left bicep. He leads this other me straight out the front doors and unhands him in the parking lot. I follow behind. I feel the cold glass window on my hand, but the two women standing near the entrance podium don't seem to notice.

"Just walk it off, 'kay, bud?"

Standing nearby is a man, one arm crossed over his chest, the other hand limp and holding a cell phone to his face. He leans heavily on one hip and looks impatient, meek, and nervous. His nerves seem to grow as the drunk man approaches, his shoulders hunched forward in a wobbly but firmly planted stance.

"Nice cargo shorts, stud."

"Excuse me. I'm on the phone," he says, voice impatient, and a slight lisp on the *x* and *s*.

"And the flip-flops. You ever flip-fuck in flip-flops?"

The man, eyes wide like a globe, turns away as his fair face swells to red. The drunk man tromps after.

I walk to my car, shaking as I start it and pull out onto Jackson Lane. At the small road near the cemetery, I see

Froglegs there again as I pass. But gone is the calming glow of a translucent blue ghost. The man, red-faced and smeared in purple bruises, looks right at me. His agonized pink eyes bore straight through mine.

The drive east to Indian Hollow is quiet until the bridge comes into view, and then there's a syncopating ache in the arches of my feet. I glance from the ditch up to the shoulder of the road and stop ten yards from the start of the bridge.

A very drunk man careens his car and launches over the pallid wall. It tumbles nose to trunk several times before landing in the water, a black-and-white silhouette echoing on the waves.

I drop to my knees, my temples buried in my palms. So tempted to scream it, speak it, make it real, if only for these last few moments.

No. No, it's not true. Why would it be? They don't even allow drinks inside. This is a reservation. We're supposed to be dry these days.

But the reality now is that echoing silhouette of a car, the surface of the water unceasing in its churn under the wake of the heavy metal. I feel my forehead thud against the black tar ridge of the rumble strip.

I land on the slot machine's screen with a thud.

Overhead are more muffled voices and that same marching beat.

"You gotta quit nodding off, my brother. They *will* kick you out eventually," Diego says, patting me on the shoulder.

"I don't know why I'm so tired all of a sudden." I laugh. "I just had a whole energy drink a little while ago."

"Heh. Try working here," he said, refilling the lemonade in my Styrofoam cup. "It does things to ya. Makes your circadian clock look like a dreamcatcher."

"Actually, Mr. Moose, can I have a coffee?"

For the first time I'm noticing the last name on his name tag as he reaches for the pitcher on his drink cart.

"Sure thing. Creamer? Sugar? Sweet'N Low? Or a whole damn chocolate bar like you young guns do?"

"Black is fine. Too much of a headache to complain."

"I'll say. Don't let the guards catch you snoozin'. I mean it. If you were just a little bit whiter and older, maybe. But rules is rules for low rollers." He winks and rolls his cart away.

In front of me, the slot machine spins and takes my last fifty credits, and lucky me. The reels line up a big scattering of black sedans with chrome lining. This one is called *Little Spider Highway.*

In total, once all the free spins are tallied, I'm sitting ahead at $550.35. I cash out, and a bright blue-and-pink ticket spits out from the validator. I pocket it and walk away from the keno section, beelining to the beverage station.

It's a pink marble and rose quartz island-booth near the blackjack tables, the only part of the floor that's well lit. I grab two large cups and fill up both with coffee, priming the espresso a few pumps and then adding an ice cube to both. I find a quiet corner of their aquarium-walled food court in a booth with a table covered in a glossy resin that holds rusty coins. Some are crude and gray, with a blank face with curly hair, and others are rosier, with pressings of dragonflies, apples, cherries, and peaches. Most are labeled 7 CENTS, with the trios of 7s carrying crowns of copper alloy flames above.

I slam the coffee, one right after the other.

Diego was right about the sweet coffee. All through college, peers waited in long lines before class, several of us often taking our desks late. It was meant to keep us alert, but on the days I'd indulge, the only guarantee was a sugar crash, either in class or on one of the chairs in the lounge near the three-treadmill-and-one-pull-up-bar gym.

The coffee tastes like free coffee always tastes. It warms up my whole body, and when it's gone, I feel a cold, crawling jitter up my skin, like a fungus crawling through maze walls.

I throw away the Styrofoam cup and walk to the gift shop's beverage cooler. I can get more caffeine faster if the drink is cold.

The cold touch of the chemical cylinder feels real enough in my hand. It opens under my fingertips with that familiar *crsss-plckt*.

Even in this labyrinthine place, it tastes just as sweet as the real thing . . .

I open the second energy drink I left in the beverage holster with my fingernail, and I bring it my lips, an action as natural as any other muscle memory I could rely on right now.

I take one big drink, savoring the static burn of the chemical bubbles. The sandman titters in the seat next to me as it feels the mélange of ungodly ingredients advertised conspicuously on the can.

With my left hand, I grab the seatbelt knife from the door's accessory pocket. I flail my arm upward and plunge the window-breaker end into the sandman's iris. It sinks, deep, like the stringy first scoop into a freshly opened pumpkin, and behind it is some rankling crunch that sends convulsions through my arm. The instant discomfort of a wolf spider crawling across your hand.

I dislodge my hand, leaving the knife behind amid a discharge of muck-brown powdery ash like a disturbed mushroom spore and gobs of maroon and black blood.

"I decide when you stop playing."

I stumble out into the road. My eyes are blurry, but I see no cars in either direction.

Behind me the sound of metal ripping and clanking. I take out my wallet, dig into the mess of crinkled paper, and grip my fingertips around the red-painted quarter. It burns like a car lighter freshly removed from the socket. I throw it ahead of me, and it falls over the side of a nearby bridge into water.

The Mississippi River. Its waves churn at me like a glittering world, smiles and starlight folding in on itself. A great green eye on a green-and-blue chessboard watches me from the sky.

I run across the bridge. When I look over my shoulder, I see my car burst open, glass and metal showering the road, and the sandman emerges. He stands atop the severed head of a gigantic bald eagle. Its feathers are filthy, all the fine plumage bunched in grimy clumps, a rusty brown disc beneath where a body should've been. It opens its mouth, a dull mechanical squall bellowing out, "Where is my body, master? This is no kind of life."

The sandman stomps on the eagle's head in answer.

With eyes red and raw like blood in the snow, the eagle looks into my eyes and in his clanky drawl half-whispers to me, "Your people won't hunt me. I'm in such pain."

After the bridge there's about twenty yards between the road and city limits of Indian Hollow. I run as fast as I can, but everything around me, all directions, won't stop mixing with the river in spirals. The trees on all sides become a flat streak across the sky, a pulsing green wave, and the road ahead of my steps bubbles and spins. But in the distance, the sign stays stationary. I stumble past it as the hard clack of the eagle's beak snaps behind me. I collapse into the ditch.

When I look west, the sandman is still standing atop the severed eagle head, hovering about seven feet off the ground, watching with wide, white eyes in a shadowed face. Returning his gaze, I back away from the edge of the road. I'm just inside the city limits, according to the population sign nearby.

The sandman says nothing.

No pow-wows in Indian Hollow, Alana said. Because eagles don't fly here.

"So I think it's a safe bet to assume you're a spirit. You and the eagle both." The scratched yellow beak of the eagle opens and emits a low, breathy rumble. "Sounds like you can't follow me into town."

"You'll need to leave this land sometime. Isn't that your goal, Nameless One?" He circles his fingers around his chin and lips before licking the tips. "The taste of your dreams. Oh, they're quiet. Your sleep doesn't see them much, but their taste is of wanderlust and the poisoned air among the great villages."

It's hard to focus on the features of his face. Whether from the dizziness of the crash or the swaying of the floating eagle, every time I try to look at his face, my gaze won't stay still. And when I try to glance back to where I thought I'd made something out, like a pale wrinkled cheek, a coarse chin, or dark brown crow's feet, it feels as if I'm looking at a different person entirely. His most elusive feature, by far, is his eyes.

"Why not just walk out here, boy? Take a shortcut. It's okay. There's a lot of back roads on this reservation. New ones popping up each day through the forests. Little by little. A walking trail here, bike path there. Have you seen? There's a lot of ways to walk the land, but no road out of Indian Hollow will end without meeting me."

"I'll find one," I say, straining for focus. As he spoke, I

thought maybe I saw a bright green iris. "This is my reservation, not yours."

The sandman laughs. "Yes, I can certainly smell the forest on you. Lots of crumbled autumn leaves and maybe a few twigs. But I've been from here for a bit longer than Ojibwe boys with cell phones can comprehend. And I've met stronger *ogichidaag* than you in my travels. It'll save so much time for you to give up the spear."

"If there's time to save, there's time to spare."

"Idiotic warriors are a danger to their family. You wouldn't want to let them down, would you?"

My gaze drifts to the cloudy red eyes of the eagle, sunken deep into a face of dark, oily feathers. The glossy dome of its pupils expands and wavers like a ripple of water. Suddenly, they're less opaque, and the eyes are filled with a burst of green and gold. The features of the sandman are in focus.

The skin on his face is a quavering mass of blue-and-green splotches, like a pile of mucky seafoam on a lake shore. Then, just as quick, a harmless, doddering old man.

In his infinite gaze, dozens of blue-domed scenes erupt throughout his face. Rows and rows of blinking slot machines in a jagged-cornered and spiraling labyrinth. Employees in golden smocks and soft blue vests bringing drinks to smiling elders. Security guards patrolling halls. A bustle of others dealing cards, counting chips and hard cash, rolling dice, pulling tabs. Solid rolls of nickels popping open against countertops, plumes and plumes of gray clouds drifting above everyone's heads, trash cans filled with used matchbooks.

"Your family is nearby. Can you spot them in the crowd? I can."

My eyes dart around the display, looking for any hint of Alana and Cherie, some flash of a glossy ponytail or their amber faces, but from one glance to another, I lose track of which screen I'm looking at.

My foot slips on a grapefruit-sized rock that lay loose in the roadside gravel. I stumble, pierced with awareness of my physical space. A black-gloved hand lunges at my chest. I back away, and the sandman's grip catches the air above the edge of the tar road.

I fall on my ass and roll backward into the dead, spiky grass, my jacket catching a lot of the powered snow on the way. I gasp as I look at the black checkerboard flags on my sleeves. I flail my arms out of the jacket and throw it toward the tree line.

From the top of this ditch, I must look ridiculous.

"You're easy to distract, *gwiiwizens*. When you're done wasting time, I'll be waiting."

With a painful shriek and a thumping flutter of wings, the sandman shoots off into the winter sky, a gust of wind shaking the tree line on either side of Jackson Lane.

I lay back in the wet snow and feel it melt and steam on my red ears, the white wisp drifting in the sky. Just before the darkness comes, there's one lone white star, its rays sharp and bright.

A13——Moccasin Game Song
(Cat. no. 203, no. 144, Bull. 45)

The moccasin game is the principal form of gambling practiced by the Chippewa at the present time. In this game four bullets or balls are hidden under four moccasins. One bullet or ball is marked and it is the object of the opposing players to locate this with as few "guesses" as possible. A characteristic of moccasin game songs is rapid drumbeat with slower tempo of the voice, as in this song. The drumbeat of these songs is a strongly accented stroke followed by a very short unaccented stroke.

This is the song of a determined player. It is the only song that was recorded by Nita' miga' bo (Leader standing), and was recorded at White Earth, Minnesota, 1907—10.

nin' gagiwě'	I will go home,
niwe' nigoyan	if I am beaten,
nin' genadĭn'	after more articles
minawa' geatc' igeyan	to wager.

PART TWO

Game of Chance

I will go home,
if I am beaten,
after more articles
to wager.

—FROM *Songs of the Chippewa,*
RECORDED AND EDITED
BY FRANCES DENSMORE

Chapter 6 ☠ TOKEN

GLENN NIELAN

November 10, 2017

High Roller

Glenn Nielan brought four suitcases of clothes and camera equipment and a crate of old newspapers to his hotel room at Hidden Atlantis. He'd considered renting one of the more private cabins out in the wooded villa by the lake, in case he needed to bring a strapping young lad to bed. But as the winter loomed over the next few weeks, he chose the warmth of the casino and the instant heat of the hotel room.

His window overlooked the north parking lot, with a sliver of the blue lake in the distance just beyond the tips of the mighty pines. Through his window, he could see the bright colors of the plastic slides from the water park, but his room was on a high enough floor that they didn't obstruct the view.

Back on the casino floor, the gaming host, George, and his assistant were waiting. George was a man in a sleek navy suit, of a similar age to Glenn, but his gelled hair and unlined face gave him a somewhat artificial youthfulness. He was objectively handsome, but a decade or two past Glenn's radar.

"Put 'er there, buddy!" George said, extending his arm. "Glad to finally get you back up here."

"Glad to finally be back," Glenn said.

The choice of words in and of themselves felt insincere, but he truly did feel a growing sense of joy. To be back among the woods, the lakes, and the electronic whirs, bells, and beeps of the slot machines. It'd been too long since he'd been to a casino that had class. Not the paltry community bingo centers for the elderly in his corner of the state. At only forty-six, Glenn refused to put any further strain on his feelings of aging by joining in those sad establishments. He'd take an Indian casino, where the history and energy was bright and youthful, even if the majority of the patrons were not.

George's assistant was a strikingly gorgeous Indian woman whose name tag said ALANA. She also wore a suit that complemented her figure quite well, but instead of a tie she had a silky pink ascot with blue seashells adorning the cloth in fine embroidery.

"We've got a whole new array of bells and whistles for you to check out, *mon frère*," George said. "What's it been, twelve years?"

"Sounds about right, yeah. Back when it had that boring name."

"And no poker tables!" George threw his head back and chuckled. "Can you even fathom a casino without poker anymore?"

"There wasn't a water park either. Actually, I might wanna check that out before sitting down for cards. It looks crazy fun from my window."

"Oh, it's the been the pride and joy of our rez for the last decade," Alana said. "If you like it, you may not end up spending a dime on the floor."

"Oh, I don't know about that much," Glenn said. "I'm here to score big. Both cash and footage."

"Footage?" Alana said. "I'm afraid we can't allow any un-approved filming inside the premises."

George put his hand on her left shoulder. "Oh no, not that kind of footage, Alana. We got us a ghost hunter here."

"Oh, well, how about that," Alana said, smiling warmly. "We've got a fair few of those around here."

"You're underselling me, George. It's not just the paranor-mal. I've got a lot of ideas for documentary footage in the area."

As a child, Glenn grew up around the northern Minnesota area, same class as George in Waubajeeg, and it'd been his dream since undergrad to come back someday and make a name for himself. After his divorce when he was thirty-five, having finally mustered the guts to tell his wife he was into men, he'd wanted to jump head on into making that dream come true.

In an accordion folder, secured tightly to the outside of his camera equipment with some length of plain twine, were dozens of articles from across Minnesota, the highs and lows, loves and grievous losses around the area. To him, a land of loss was ripe for capturing a story worth showing.

Or a land of loss, the state itself, with a scattering of old tuberculosis hostels and secluded sanitariums, could at the very least make for a thrilling ghost-hunting show. And with the luck and splendor of a place like Atlantis, he knew he had it in him to make it all happen.

The two hosts led him from the floor to the entrance of the water park, where the thick and humid smell of chlorine assaulted his nose. His flip-flops provided no sort of protec-tion as he walked across the soaked tiles, but the sight of the park itself was so breathtaking he didn't care about wet socks.

There were two moats, one a small play area for young

children, and the second, a larger lazy river for tubing, surrounding a small castle with white, Greek-styled pillars, with three fountains spraying water over the tops of the castle's three spires. From a distance, the outline of the structure looked like a trident. The two outer spires were topped with a lustrous plastic sun and moon, the moon a cream-colored crescent and the sun a wavy orange starfish. The three waterslides swirled above the castle, not unlike a ribbon of DNA, and their spouts launched children into three pools of various depths, the largest of which was also a gently churning whirlpool.

A chemically treated water paradise. Glenn was in total awe.

"Believe it or not," George said as he patted Glenn's shoulders, "that's not even the most beautiful part of the casino. In this white man's opinion, at least."

"It's a marvel, for sure," Alana said. "But a little too Mediterranean to feel like home."

"If it's not too chilly fer ya, we can head outside and see the mural."

On the outside of the casino on a gray wall, a colorful scene had been painted, with dozens of artists' signatures scrawled about the edges. The symbols included the usual tribal motifs, animals, medicine wheels, feathers, and the like. Glenn's favorite was what appeared to be an Indigenous depiction of the Virgin Mary and her husband Joseph, both looking down at a shining golden orb at their feet.

"Are there a lot of religious Indians still?" Glenn asked George.

"Yeah, pretty much. We're inclusive here."

"Yeah, yeah, sure."

"We've got a little joke going at the tribal council. They call these two the Venerated Helen and Russell."

"But where's Jesus?"

"Who knows? I think the artist wasn't good at drawing babies, and no one was real eager to add even more religiosity to the walls. So far as I'm concerned, all they're looking at is a pot of gold."

Nearby on the impeccably green lawn in front of the bay windows were two statues of well-antlered bucks. From the bay windows, the water park was visible inside, the three slides swirling above the lawn and the deer statues on thick stilts before looping back inside to the chlorine depths.

"Simply beautiful," Glenn said, the lights of the parking lot gleaming in his eyes. "And it pays for itself, really."

While George led him back inside, Glenn discreetly checked the grids of his dating app. He saw no sign of the boy he'd tried to connect with earlier on the casino floor, but no matter. By the look of the grid, there would be no shortage of warriors about.

100 Credits

Later, in the early hours of twilight, after he bade farewell to his courteous hosts, Glenn attempted to cash in the one-dollar casino token he'd kept hidden in his closet for nigh on a decade, but he was rebuffed at the cashier's counter. The token was old, from years before the remodel turned the Waubajeeg Community Casino to the current Greek paradise in late 2008. It didn't even have a good aesthetic to it; the tails side was a simple $1, neither symbol in a serif font, and the other side was a simple seal of wheat surrounding the initials WCC.

"I'm sorry, sir, but the grace period to cash in this token ended years ago," the cashier told him. "I can't exchange this."

"Forgive me for being rude, but that's some horseshit. I was never told this would expire."

"I've never even seen this kind before. I was only a kid when WCC was open."

Glenn sighed. He didn't want to approach this young employee in anger. Instead, he opted for a different tactic.

"Forgive my rudeness. It's just that . . . this belonged to my wife. She loved gambling here. But—but I forced her to exclude herself because she was spending way too much money . . . then she died a few years ago. This was one of the things she had in her purse, and I wanted to give her one last go here. Maybe spend that dollar on her favorite machine."

The young cashier nodded, face calm, nonreactive, and exchanged the coin, handing over a crisp dollar noticeably slowly.

Glenn smiled, winked, and beelined it to the penny slot machines, where he had to wait a few minutes before a good seat freed up. It was a simple game, *Crazy Cash Cave*, some birds, some cherries, 7s, and triple bars, and he watched the hundred credits play ten rounds down to zero. None of his bets won, and the last part of his late wife that had value to him spun down the reels.

No one ever had a painless life, he thought. *At least you can rest painless now, darling wife.*

Now that the token, or at least the credit he'd been able to claim for it, was lost to the churn of random numbers on the screen, Glenn wanted to leave, but instead, he pulled out his wallet. What was a few more twenties, especially for Tiff's favorite machine?

A hundred dollars or a hundred spins later, the attendants were bringing him another jackpot. For a moment he'd wondered if perhaps they really did turn the machines up for his visit. The jackpot was $535.53. Wasn't that the same exact amount he'd won when trying to romance the first boy from the atrium? The thought of it made him instinctively reach for his phone again.

He took a deep, cigarette-scented breath as he pocketed his winnings. He was up nearly ten thousand dollars in his first day. A type of high he couldn't find any other way but to spend.

The Later Lovers of Orpheus

He sipped a scotch with ice at the pink-and-gold bar counter near the edge of the casino floor. Every barstool had a golden vinyl cover, the seams a sparkly silver wrapped in a clear plastic. The lights above were dimmed, but each corner of the bar counter had a small, round lamp made of clay with electric lighting under a false oil wick made of stained glass. Everything about the casino atmosphere warmed his bones as the winter set in.

The first snowstorm had come just three days before Halloween, but it'd been dry the first few weeks in November. The casino was prepping for Thanksgiving, the employees wearing broaches of cornucopias and red turkey feathers, the peppy bartender talking him into ordering their special dinner prepared for the casino floor in two days. Glenn was hoping to indulge the company of an interesting young man, maybe even fall in love, while he waited for approval of his documentary from the bigger managers. The past few weeks he'd not done or heard much since the first day when George had rolled out a great welcome.

In the interim, a grid of men on his phone kept him company, sometimes in person.

hey there handsome. What brings you this far north?

Glenn was all too eager to respond. *Here to serve my queen, Lady Luck. She's been good to daddy.*

This first boy he met was two towns north of Waubajeeg, a little village called The Fox's Roost. Glenn offered to pick the lad up, but he insisted on waiting for public transportation.

It'll take me about an hour to get there, maybe hour and a half if the driver's late.

Lol why would the driver be late? Glenn responded.

Because of Jack.

Jack?

Jack Daniels. :P

LOL that's funny. I know the guys who run this place, they wouldn't let that happen.

Still. Hour and a half, probably.

Long way to wait without a picture.

A young Native man's face appeared, with an array of tattooed arrows wrapping around his right eye like a nautilus shell, snaking down toward his earlobe like a top-heavy *S*.

Handsome young lad. How about his body?

A torso, slender and smooth, with a bumpy abdomen like a ridged bar of caramel.

What daddy likes to see. You play hockey?

The boy's profile name was Puck, and in his faceless photo he wore a forest-green-and-brown jersey, number 02.

Used to. Got crowded out by bigger guys as I got older.

Can't wait to see your body in action. ;) How close are you, Puck?

The bus is almost to Waubajeeg. Be there soon, cousin.

Cousin?

Ten minutes passed, Glenn growing anxious with each, and he sent a second message. *COUSIN??*

The boy's profile was offline.

Glenn threw back his drink, ordered a beer, and slunk away to one of the big progressive machines, one with five-digit figures dangling above the players' heads in a tall, curved screen. He threw in fifty dollars, lit a cigarette, and then heard the notification bell of his app of prospects.

I'm at the water slide, where r u?

Water slide?? WHY?

To swim, why else.

I'm not in swim clothes, silly boy.

Get some, and we'll try out the slides.

Meet me at my room? I'll change.

Ok.

He sent his hotel room number to the lad and cashed back out his fifty dollars, the reels having sought fit to reward him with thirty-three more cents after a few spins had brought him down, down, and then trickled back up. He stuffed the ticket into his back pocket, slammed the second drink, and strode off toward the hotel hallways.

Puck waited for him at the door. He had a short and wiry frame in loose clothes: jeans that looked three sizes too big, slip-on loafers made of cheap pleather, and a billowy blue shirt with its buttons undone, revealing the tall lines of a white tank top. His body matched the pics from what Glenn could see. A meek but curious and friendly freckled face. A curious little muskrat, wandering out of the marsh and into a land of bells and whistles and secondhand stale air.

"You're slow," the boy said with a grin.

"Come on in."

He brought Puck inside, and quickly he was poking about around the second bed and far corner table, where Glenn's array of suitcases, cameras, laptops, tablets, lamps, and boom mics were stacked across that half of the room.

"Preparing for a concert?"

"No, a documentary."

"About what?"

"This land that I love," Glenn said as he wrapped his arms around Puck from behind. "The ghosts hiding in the woods and streams and rivers."

"You live here? You seem like an out-of-towner."

"How's that?"

"You're still wearing shorts and sandals."

"These clothes don't feel much heavier," he said, running his hand across the boy's chest.

"Indian skin," the boy said, his hands taking ahold of Glenn's wrists and gently pulling out of his grip. "You can tell me more about your movie while you change. Don't worry. The door is thin."

He was right. Glenn slipped off a red satin jock and threw on a pair of long, blue swim trunks. He took off his polo and slipped on a dark-purple Vikings T-shirt with the sleeves cut off.

"I realize I should've asked you this sooner, but you're over age, right?"

"Of course," Puck said as the thin, white door slid open. "Why wouldn't I be?"

"You sure don't look drink-buyin' age, cutie."

"I'm old enough to buy drinks."

"Care to prove it?" Glenn winked as he approached Puck. "Not that I don't trust you, but I was in the middle of a drink. And a winning streak on that game."

He nodded. "Sure. I'll buy."

The boy smiled at him, and Glenn felt his ears tingle with red and his heart the pace of an island drum, but thankfully Puck turned away and slipped into the hall without noticing. They walked together, through the camera'd halls of the hotel and the casino floor, eyes of plastic and of flesh all around, but the only eyes that mattered to him were Puck's, who continued to give him short, small glances up as they walked around the bar.

"Two Mermaid Castles, please."

"Sure thing, sir," the young woman said as she ran Puck's ID through her till.

"That's how teen girls drink," Glenn said with a laugh. "Mature men go for whiskey." He turned back to the waitress. "I'll take a menu, too, please."

The girl prepped the drinks while Glenn ordered a side glass of whiskey and a plate of beef Stroganoff noodles. Puck giggled. "I prefer sweet to the tongue." The woman handed them each a frothy blue drink in a wavy tropical glass, topped with a cone of light-blue whipped cream and three spotted-blue wafer cookies stacked like a teepee over the foam. "And sound to the eye." He bit into the cookie and winked.

They finished what Glenn privately dubbed the worst frou-frou monstrosity of his life, an ungodly mix of artificial blueberry and buttercream, and then bought two shots of honey whiskey.

"I promise it's sweet enough. Child, you're gonna give me diabetes watching you if you order another."

They clinked glasses and then found themselves on the threshold of the water park.

Its four plastic spires all emitted neon, backlit streams of water, each arched tall and thin like a clamshell as the spray fell onto a moat of shallow water and soft floating toys for the younger kids. The three large slides twirled above it all, each ending in a different section of three surrounding pools, which all together was only half the size of the wave pool beyond.

"I wanna go to the big slide," Puck said. "How about you, old man?"

"Hey now. I'm not that much older than you," he said.

"Then follow me."

Puck took off his shirt, giving Glenn a glance at the same shapely torso from the photo, and led him around the edge of the outer pool behind the castle, and they walked up a set of stairs made of white diamond-grated metal, with three landings for the respective slide entrances. They climbed to the purple landing, the tallest slide.

"Do you have any waterproof cameras?" Puck said as he sat in the front of a two-seated inflatable raft, a black mesh net over a dark purple sheen.

"A GoPro but not on me. The slide looks pretty dark, though." A dark mouth gaped at the end of the landing, torrents of chlorinated water diving into the chasm.

"How about some of those ghost-hunting cameras?"

Glenn sat in the back, and Puck settled in between his thighs as the park attendant stood behind them both to push. Puck giggled when he leaned back a few inches. It was a good thing they were headed into the dark.

Sloshing and moist, rushing wind greeted the pair as they shot down into the dark spiral. Glenn giggled softly through his nose, but the boy screamed and war-whooped like a cute little cartoon character. When the golden light returned as the raft launched from the mouth of the slide to the catch-pool, Puck turned around and smiled. *A doe-eyed boy smiling for me*, Glenn thought.

"Again?"

"As many as you'd like, cutie."

"Let's check out the others."

They returned to the white stairs, second landing and then first, the trip through the dark slower, or so it seemed to Glenn. The third seemed rather tame to him, but his soon-to-be paramour had an unsure look of fright on him.

"Did you see her?"

"What?"

"There was a ghost in the tunnel."

"You fucking with me?"

Puck laughed, his look of fright loosening to a nervous calm. "No, I'd never."

Glenn placed the raft back in the pile with the others. "I don't think I'm privy to that sort of thing. What did she look like?"

"I only saw her for like a second. She had dark hair and a lot of makeup on her eyes. Like the Cleopatra machine over in Noddingham."

"Do you mean *Pharaoh's Bedroom* or *Grandeur of the Nile*?"

"Ooh, that's what it's called? I never really know them by name." The boy winked. "Just the pictures. But yeah, how she's standing in that one, that's what the ghost looked like."

"Huh."

Glenn walked over to the table, toweled off, and slipped on his shirt. Puck followed. "Do you want to go play on those machines?"

"I don't know if we'll be able to get seats. Noddingham's usually full these days."

"We'll find a spot. It's easy enough."

Glenn heard the padding footsteps behind him, but his attention was only ahead of him as the automatic doors with white flowery decals opened and led to the casino floor.

At a small machine with an older style, a faded printed vinyl showed an exoticized portrayal of Cleopatra, a light-bronze seductress with a stenciled cage of black eyeliner surrounding a piercing gaze. The plastic sign above the screen said CLEOPATRA'S COINS.

Tiff always loved this machine. The days when their marriage was easiest, their eyes only focused on the reels delivering stacks of gold, sphinxes, glyphs, and a small sketch of a basket in a reedy river, all surrounded by a dull white backlight behind each spin.

"I don't have my wallet," he said to Puck as the boy caught up. "I'll need to go back to my room to get some cash."

Puck sighed. "Oh. I guess I didn't really wanna gamble today. I wanted to go on the lazy river."

"I know, but kid, I got a good feeling about this machine."

"Maybe we could meet up later? When you're done?"

"Sure, bud."

The boy's eyes narrowed and peered through him, until finally a playful smile emerged. "You be on your best behavior, young man. Make good choices."

"That's my line, boy."

He scampered away, and Glenn went back to his room. He slipped on a drier pair of swim trunks and grabbed his wallet. It sat on a stack of two plain office storage boxes, each filled with copies of the *Geshig Herald* and the *Waubajeeg Times*. Some gifts from his mother, whose second marriage to a member of the reservation brought them from Apple Valley to Languille Lake in his youth, and many more from Tiffany, whom he'd met in Waubajeeg High School and married just before college.

A box filled with history, waiting to be documented, to bring the dead back to life again, through his lens and his care.

I hope you're proud, Tiff. I know you would be.

Back at the casino, he withdrew several hundred dollars and sat at the machine again. Every so often the sphinxes appeared in the right numbers and order to trigger the bonus, and an animation of a gold coins, dishes, vases, and cat statues rained while the digital credits below steadily raised.

It was hours before he realized the boy wasn't coming back, and he knew that he wouldn't find him again on the screen, but there would be plenty of others. The faint light of the casino entrance, the blue daylight, grew just a little darker and dimmer each evening. When it's cold, the puppies come inside.

And they come to me, he thought as the jackpot finally triggered.

A Native man with a drink cart congratulated him and handed him a small cup of tropical fruit from under a cloth-covered basket. He bit down on a squishy orange cube of papaya and waited for his prize.

Chapter 7 ☠ MANDATORY VACATION

ALANA BULLHEAD

November 26, 2017

"I t's okay to stop worrying, babe."

Zach's big hands settled on Alana's shoulders delicately, and she felt her ponytail come loose as he rubbed his nose into the side of her head, a small breath of air tickling her earlobes, his hand reaching for her womb.

"Get off me," she said, brushing him off with her right shoulder. "We're not that far from the floor."

She'd been standing at the end of the hallway that connected the hotel hallway, the water park, and the casino floor through a big, echoing lounge. There were few places in the building where there weren't some eyes of white or in shadow watched. And Zach was turning into a sugary wuss more and more with every day that passed since she'd told him about the baby.

"Your worrying is gonna start making me worry. I want you to relax before your vacation," he said.

"Will be nothing relaxing about it. I'll be worrying about this place every day."

"Ah, c'mon, babe. We'll be fine without you."

She laughed so soft and half-heartedly, like a baby's snore, that what she said came out much colder than she meant: "Real reassuring coming from some security guard."

The offense in Zach's eyes was instant. "Oh, I'm so sorry I care about you getting rest for our baby. Must be devasting." He finally turned away from her. "And we keep this place you're so attached to safe."

"You know I didn't mean that," she said. Instinctively, she took a step toward him and wanted to lean against his body, put two hands on his shoulder, and hope for a loving gaze returned.

But they were still in view of the cameras.

"I just don't want you to stay as stressed as you do, babe. This place can run fine without you, and if they can't, they're gearing up for failure anyway. Plus, that cousin of yours won't even text back. That's on him, not you."

She took another step toward him, this time more defiant. "Look, I know you don't like Liam, but I asked you nicely to get off his back!"

Zach groaned and pushed his eyebrows up with the bottom of his hands. "No, not your bestie Liam. The other one, the little fairy boy who won the jackpot."

"Oh." She blushed. "I think he's just spacey. He'll get back to me when he can."

"And don't worry. I know perfectly well how protective you are of Liam. We all know." He stomped away without looking back, fading into the rows of slot machines until only his pretty yellow hair was visible.

Maybe she did prefer the sugar-wuss version of him.

*

There was only an hour of work left before her mandatory time off officially started, and even though she was behind on paperwork, her friend Bella promised to take care of it for her. A few months before, Alana had covered for her coworker to George when she was going through a particularly bad week and ended up erroneously reimbursing machine credits to a couple of guests. Bella's work outside of that incident was punctual and reliable, so Alana was not worried. She spent the last hour on shift wandering the floor, making small talk with employees and guests, on the lookout for anything abnormal.

In a casino, the bar for abnormal can fluctuate, and today it felt higher than usual. As did many guests. Lots and lots of glazed eyes, wobbly necks and shoulders, and loud laughs that follow inebriation. It was three in the afternoon, and several parties had already started. College kids from Half Lake, rapping and calling at the blackjack tables; a group of grizzled men around a long poker table, all with golf polos that looked like they came from Walmart; and a few small groups of Native women with too-big sweaters and too-small jeans, swaying across the floor in giddy giggles.

Alana stopped at the north beverage station, where the whole of the casino area, from wall to wall, could be seen, though everything on the floor obscured the view in a maze of black plastic, red velvet ropes with gold chains, and neon screens. Patrons drifted back and forth, in and out between the banks, in big clouds of cigarette smoke that had begun staining the beautiful golden ceiling into a dingy bronze in some areas with less vents.

As she stared at the sea of dim lights and smoke, a headache slithered its way across her forehead, down around both temples, finally settling above her eyes. But apart from the blur of astigmatic intersections, nothing in front of her was outside of normal reality. No brilliant fires dancing on the corners of her eyes, no spiral patterns that ghosts left in their wake, no chills on her skin, no fever under it, no distortions to be seen.

She scowled. It had never been this hard to call on her aunt's sevenfire sight for guidance. She'd learned it at thirteen, and only now at twenty-eight, her life officially longer with the sight than without, it failed.

A smile in the crowd seemed to respond to her scowl. A pale face across the floor, standing perfectly between a row of machines so he could be spotted. An old man. But was it the same?

Without her sight, there was little chance of finding out. Alana still recoiled remembering the few times she'd seen him in the past year. A different face each time, but there was no mistaking the ripples in the air when he walked by, translucent and orange through the sevenfire gaze.

For a whole minute, the old man kept staring and smiling.

She tried to walk out of his view and block his visage behind a slot machine, but every time she moved away from the beverage station, his face stayed centerfield. Those glowering nickel-ball eyes glued to her every movement, a crooked smile like a paisley teardrop ending at his ears.

Soon, her legs grew too heavy to keep walking, and her neck locked into place.

The writhing bustle of the patrons at their seats and the dancing lights seemed to swirl around the sandman's face like a vile pow-wow grand entry. She thought she heard the drummers now, playing in the crowd, but realized it was her heart. She brought her hands to her stomach.

Coward. Only showing your face when my sight is weak.

The ghost-stale air of the casino suddenly whipped like a storm, and in an instant the sandman's face flew in next to her own, a rough, breathy laugh shaking in her ear like a turtle shell's rattle.

Coward? When did you see me cower, girl? I may not seem as eager for play as you, but let this remind you I hold the better odds.

Her vision returned with the static crunch of a radio.

"Hold on, Alana. We've got a medic on the way!"

"What?"

She felt her body slumped against the navy-gold carpet while the guard knelt above her protectively, fanning air to her face with a slot promotions brochure.

"Do you need some water?"

"I'm good, Jack. Really, thank you."

"Alana!"

Zach came bounding from somewhere on the west floor and collapsed next to her. "Babe, what happened?"

She took a few quick breaths and stood up. "I'm fine. Lightheaded. Need more water."

"Okay, sweetie. Anything."

As he picked up a cardboard cup of water from the beverage fountain, the on-site medic arrived. He had her follow a thin flashlight with her eyes, and then she sipped at the water while they escorted her to the medical station at the back of the house.

After a quick vital check by the medic, Alana peed in a cup, a simple formality should any paperwork need to be submitted to insurance.

"Sorry, kiddo. The rapid screen is positive for THC . . . and opiates? Oh, Alana . . ."

Her mouth fell agape, and she wanted to respond, *No, obviously impossible. Do another.*

Then she remembered the voice on the wind.

I have the better odds, girl.

She dropped her forehead into her palms and waited for her boss to come talk to her about another mandatory vacation.

Chapter 8 ☠ NIGHTMARE IN THE NORTHWOODS

CHERIE HALTSTORM

December 4, 2017

"Buckle up, junkie," Cherie said as Alana stepped into her car.

"Not funny," her cousin said, flicking at the pine-scented air-freshener and red handprint medallion that dangled from Cherie's rearview mirror. She pulled the bottom of the fake pine tree until the elastic snapped back and wrapped around the back of the mirror. "My whole vacation week was ruined."

"Eh, you were already dreading it, according to Zach." Her cousin's baby daddy was eager to force Alana to get some rest, and the vacation requirement for PTO hoarders meant he had help from management to manage the woman he couldn't.

"But in my own way, and that didn't include having to come back in the middle for a retest."

"You pass that one?"

"Of course!"

"Hey, I won't judge if you've been sneaking some of Liam's stash. Or Auntie's."

Alana tried to scoff at her but it came out a snort and a laugh. "They'd both love that. I know it."

"What'd Georgie say about the second test?"

"He's cool. At first, he was all disappointed and stuff, but now he's sure the first was a false positive. I'm no longer off the schedule."

"How's your baby daddy taking the news?"

"So far, Zach's buying the false positive explanation, but before that he thought maybe I'd been hanging around Liam too much."

"Seriously?"

"Yup. He stopped short of accusing Liam of drugging me, but I know he wanted to, so I made him walk away."

Cherie hid her anger as best she could. Where Liam had made a quick enemy of Zach with his wayward chemical odyssey, Cherie had the coworker camaraderie, along with her connection to Alana, to help Zach look past her own. She'd been sober for eight years, with the love of her sister to guide her through that old summer storm.

"Why do you think the sandman did it?"

"A warning. He knows we're on to him, and he knows the baby's been weakening my sight. He wants us to stop chasing him."

"Any word back from Marion?"

"None. Not from him or from his mother. I thought he was expected down in the cities, but no one seems to realize he's not around."

Cherie let the silence linger between them before talking. "Probably just partying if he's our cousin." The men in all three of their family branches had a bad habit of disappearing after parties, whether to the open road or immovable graves. *Here's hopin' you're a little wiser, cousin.*

Alana laughed. "Oh, we'll find him. And we'll put an end to that old man before winter. I can feel it."

*

While Nielan was waiting to hear back from the tribe, George had tasked Cherie and Alana with keeping him occupied and entertained. She'd been sitting in the break room at work, seeing her cohorts engaged in paranormal investigation shows, when the idea came to her. Cherie proposed they take Nielan on a ghost hunt. The old Johnston Hostel for Tuberculosis was fourteen miles southeast of Waubajeeg, on a winding tar road that led to a winding dirt road that led to a dead end.

Just like this guy's dreams, Cherie thought as she rifled through the newspapers on his bed. Before he moved to one of the lakeshore cabins behind the casino, Glenn was in a hotel room, spending his nights flirting it up with dainty little Native guys, paying for their drinks and giving them slot machine money. He was tight-lipped about his investments but a nauseating braggart about how much he'd spent on his cameras. When Glenn wasn't looking, some of the guards double-checked his boy toys' licenses for hints of fraud, to no avail but pissing them off. As far as her department was concerned, the fancy little filmmaker only liked men who he could buy drinks for but who typically didn't look like it.

Who am I to judge, though? I've dated grosser straight men. "How many years back do you got?" she asked.

"About sixty," Glenn said as he fixed a pot of coffee in the lake cabin's kitchenette. "Mostly the eighties through today, though."

"You grew up around here, *chimook*?"

"For middle and high school, yeah. Always loved the area,

but me and Tiff moved to the cities for college. We worked
our way back here every year or so. Couple of times a year,
maybe." His fingers tapped on the dark blue tabletop as he
talked about his ex-wife. "Always made sure to get a copy of
the paper from my folks when I could. Sometimes she'd do the
same, but she forgot a lot too."

"So what are you doing with them?"

"They're the basis of my project. I submitted a request
from the tribe to endorse and maybe even finance a documentary series about Languille Lake's efforts to move through the
darkness of modern life."

"Uh-huh . . ."

Cherie stopped when she found the paper that contained
her brother's name.

"Nightmare in the Northwoods."

A party gone wrong, but such a lifetime ago, she thought,
her breath stifled by the sudden tightness in her throat. Her
older brother, her uncle, and four other friends from across
the reservation, all stricken by a batch too strong. She'd only
been thirteen when the article came out. Faces of the family
she would never see again, splayed across the grainy circles of
the state's largest newspaper. Thousands of words, all about
what darkness awaits the people who travel north of the Twin
Cities to Indian Country.

I could take it, she thought. *But he could have copies. Or a
working phone.*

She set the newspaper down and put the cover back on
the box of dry, gray stacks. Then she cleared her throat and
turned back to the jumpy manlet.

"Your car or mine, bud?"

"We'll need my truck to bring some of the equipment.
Don't worry. You and your cousin will both fit."

Twenty minutes later, Glenn's truck pulled onto the spiraling road, where the gaps in the trees to the southwest showed the freezing lake and Hidden Atlantis on the farther shore.

Cherie helped Glenn unload his equipment and haul it into the front entrance of the Johnston Hostel. It smelled like mold and what she thought might be some faint human odor, but mostly it all smelled cold. Every window was either smashed out completely or shattered, with many doors torn straight off their hinges, and some of the walls had massive holes that looked like a hammer or an ax was taken to the wood.

Rez kids for sure. She smirked, recalling the memory of breaking the windows with rocks when she'd last been there. At least a decade ago, right around fifteen, when her sadness for her brother morphed from slow melancholia to a drive for action and destruction. It was in the last remaining days of childhood sobriety, before the next five years of her life spiralized into a fast-paced party haze.

Before they arrived, Alana had Zach plow the snow from the trail and the lawn area in front of the hostel. Cherie found Alana pacing around, staring up at the darker but still mostly shattered windows on the higher floors.

"What's up, my girl? Finding anyone for duder to interview?"

A puff of frustrated steam escaped through her red scarf. "No. Nothing. Nothing's here, sis."

Cherie could hear the mix of anger, confusion, and fear in her cousin's voice. More than anything before in her life, this was making Cherie uncomfortable in a sort of superlunary way. Something beyond her own years of skepticism, a feeling that hadn't welled within her since before her brother Rheon's death.

Before the feeling could swell more, she pushed down the fear and put her arm around Alana's shoulder. "It'll come back, *nimisehn*."

"It really doesn't feel like it, Cherie. Honestly, I've never felt so damn blind before. This place could've never seen a single death or even human presence here. That's what it feels like. I don't like this." She wiped away a tear. "Let's just wait for the *chimook* to tire himself out and get away from here."

"I'm all for that. You gonna fake a little of the spirit stuff to get him riled?"

Alana laughed. "As long as it keeps him occupied. Seems like the type to just run with whatever the mystical *niiji*s say."

Glenn stopped at the front entrance with his hands in his pockets. "We should make an offering," he called back. "To let the spirits know we're no threat."

Cherie and Alana resisted the urge to laugh at his words until he pulled from his pocket a vibrant red-and-yellow disc. A bingo chip from a bygone era, before Atlantis rose. Cherie recognized it from a shift where she and a few other guards were the signing witnesses to their destruction. By her first job at age twenty, bingo fever on the rez had faded, and as with all fading things, cleanup was needed. She thought she'd seen the last of them go through a hydraulic shredder.

Glenn kissed the coin before setting it on the first windowsill to the right of the front door.

Cherie looked at Alana and saw her cousin locked in stern concentration. Glenn turned back to them, and Alana's face changed to soft and cordial just as quick. "Might I ask you about that?" she said.

"It's no problem. My wife loved bingo and coin collecting. Now that she's done with it, I figure the best thing to do is bring it home."

Alana's customer service smile dropped into a more amused one. "Mr. Nielan, I don't know if you're gonna see much action tonight. Ghosts don't tend to haunt the ones that show respect."

"Are you saying I should be more disrespectful, Ms. Bullhead?" the man giggled.

"Just a suggestion," Alana said with a shrug. "I have to admit, I'm still in the dark about what kind of tone you're looking for."

Glenn laughed, hoisted his camera onto his shoulder, and grabbed the door handle. "I can figure that out later."

"What happened?" Cherie whispered when he was out of earshot.

"Nothing yet, but didn't you feel that when he set the token down? It was like the whole building was invited to come to life again."

She sighed. "Nah, still nothing on my end, cousin."

"Well, keep that up when we go inside in case he invited something worse than a ghost with a cough."

*

Not five steps into the hostel, Alana's concern for the spirits fled with the buzz of her phone. Cherie watched her pull the green circle to yellow beneath Zach's face and begin what she knew was an aggressive text about not disturbing her. "Go on. I'll catch up."

Cherie walked into a filthy hallway, lit by the lamps the baby daddy took care of earlier. As she glanced into dark rooms where he hadn't hung any lamps, she felt a reflexive chill and reminded herself to send him a thank-you text for doing so much for something he took no more seriously than she did.

Under her foot, a piece of dry particle board crumbled. She felt the crunch, but it must have been too damp or spongy inside to make a noise. Cherie looked back at the orange cage of the hanging lamp. No electric buzz.

Somewhere outside, she knew there was a gas generator that Zach had set up to power their expedition, but it occurred to her only just then that she'd never consciously heard it running.

Not a whir of an engine, not the clattering shake of oil-black metal. Above and all around her, the dilapidated building allegedly held the weight of history, but the old bones of dead consumption victims were just as silent as the peeling walls. Cherie couldn't hear creaks or pops, no footsteps, not the howling winter wind of the lake outside, not a car on the highway on an evening early enough to be heavy with traffic.

Finally, a sound.

Cherie heard Glenn's voice through the sanatorium's Swiss-cheese walls.

"Puck? What are you doing here?"

"You good, Nielan?" she said as she walked through the hall and into the ward from which his voice had echoed.

He turned to her with big, confused eyes, paler than his resting complexion except for his nose, reddened and running from the cold.

"Uh, yeah. Yeah, no, just looking at these marks where all these beds used to be. Some good visuals, nice and spooky."

"Who's Puck?"

"No clue."

"I thought I heard you yell at someone named Puck."

"Oh. Oh no, sorry. I said Fuck. Ah, fuck, who goes there? Ya know, for the climax at the end of the episode. I think we can retrofit something around it."

Cherie usually looked to Alana if something like this went on, but with her sense apparently dampened, she'd likely be no more help than herself.

"You seem a little rattled."

Nielan huffed one small laugh and leaned against the wall. "I must sound like I'm high."

"Nah, I know high, and you just sound scared and exhausted. All tuckered out already?"

"Maybe I should be high," Glenn said, reaching for a pack of cigarettes in his coat pocket. "Wouldn't be hard to find it around here."

"Not my lane, Nielan. But you're right. I could find it for you without even trying."

"Why not your lane?"

"Responsibilities. Bills. Ya know."

"I know."

"Been tempting, though," Cherie said, thinking of dopey young Liam, flopping about the rez, lost and numb. She'd have smoked him up years ago if he'd been old enough. "Your poison?"

"Little of this, little of that." Glenn shrugged.

Cherie could hear Alana's footsteps approaching from the hallway. "If you need a little of this or that to calm those nerves, you have my number."

"Gotcha."

Alana's head swiveled back and forth toward the ceiling as she walked in. "Oh, those are some auras, for sure."

"Maybe we'll come back for them," Glenn said. "My equipment is getting cold. And I guess I'm not really feeling the magic today."

They walked back to her truck, Glenn back to his normal excitement, already spilling his next filming ideas to Alana.

"I'm thinking maybe something inside the casinos. Ya know, really show off all the work you guys did in the remodel."

"No," they said in unison.

"Absolute hard no," Alana stressed. "No cameras inside."

On the drive back, Cherie remembered the bingo token and for a moment wished she'd checked the windowsill to see if it was still there.

Chapter 9 ♧ BAD MEDICINES

ZACH OSTLUND

December 16, 2017

He'd been switching between shifts for so many months now, it was hard to tell daylight from the fluorescent hallways or the hallways from the burning light of a cell phone at night, when Alana wasn't home.

Going on two years now, he was only just starting to settle with this new life, so different now from the Zach who'd moved to the area for a carpentry degree. One part-time security job and two semesters later, he had family on the way.

It was the exact sentiment his mother had wished for him, as had his aunts, uncles, and two younger sisters. He'd been insistent from the beginning on finishing his degree without further commitment. His walk and heart rate were faster lately, and he was privately in awe of how the tables had turned so swiftly.

He was only on his third day of Alana's vacation and already too anxious to be 100 on the floor and in class, as he'd always been.

Now the casino floor danced in a blur before him, a gray wind of customers and cigarette smoke, bells and whistles, laughs and whoops, and the wheels of the food carts, always a row or two away. Every so often, he ducked a corner or two, where no one on ground, sea, or sky could spot him, and plucked out the phone on his belt to check for a word from Alana.

Still nothing beyond a wink and heart.

How's baby?

exhausting! accompanied by a sleepy face.

He sighed, tucked the phone away, and checked his watch. It was ten minutes to 3:00 a.m., when his turn as perimeter patrol started.

He slammed two high-caffeine energy drinks, layered up—boots, gloves, mask on—and then he was out of the back doors of the casino and into the wintry parking lot.

The snowfall and wind were both modest tonight, a slow accumulation on the ground, but no icy glaze over the tar from what he could see.

Zach circled clockwise from the north and came to the road between the fenced-off waterslides and the big silver reflecting pool, the rocky shores collecting craggy piles of snow that made the whole circle of water look like a jigsaw puzzle with all the border pieces removed.

Some dark shadow of a muskrat or a beaver scurried across the surface, its intent quick and desperate for the opposite shore.

Across the reflecting pool on the opposite shore, he saw a bulky silhouette floating over the rocks. A fisherman's hat and a big wheel. The shadow looked like a man in a wheelchair. But there was no noise to accompany it, and when he squinted, the shape disappeared. Just a trick of the light, and the falling snow.

He walked to the very southeast end of the parking lot, where the cars turned out onto Jackson Lane, east to Indian Hollow and north toward Geshig.

On the shoulder of the road turning out of the parking lot to the east, he found a set of thin-wheeled tracks.

When he told his coworkers back at the security station, he sighed as the laughs he should've expected came in response.

"Sounds like someone's been chilling in the break room too long. Them ghost shows are getting to his head."

"No, it's his snag. Getting some of that Indian sight from his girl. *Neh.*"

At quarter after midnight, he walked out of the casino and to his truck. Zach saw the little imp Liam on the road when he was leaving the gas station on the north end of Waubajeeg.

Think of the irritating devil, and he'll hold out his thumb, Zach thought with audible scoff, for no one's ears or satisfaction but his own.

"Going somewheres, bud?" he said flatly as he slowed the truck and opened the passenger window.

"Yeah, back to Geshig."

"Hop in, Liam."

"I wouldn't wanna impose." He raised his arms and turned his head away at a bias with eyes closed.

"Ey now. Quit that. You're family. You'll always be family." Liam jumped in and buckled. "Even though you've been a headache on the floor."

"Thanks, bro . . . I got kicked out of the bingo van. But you probably know that already."

Zach saw two bright blue headlights approaching in the rearview, so he sped away, the truck's boom like a generator.

"Something about it might've crossed the desk, but I didn't look at it. Like I said, you'll always be family." He paused. "And since you're family, you wouldn't mind telling me what happened. I'd like to hear it from you."

Liam scoffed. "Chh. Don't try to lie. You read that shit."

"I read nothing," Zach said. "Doesn't mean I didn't hear some, but just the overview from a supervisor. C'mon, man. I'd like to hear it from where you are. Alana told me you felt judged, so I'm listening."

"That fuckin' driver lied. She said I was trafficking pills, but they were just my own prescriptions."

"What kind of scrips? If I may."

"Just my shit. I don't wanna go into it."

"My bad. Did you have the prescription paperwork with you?"

"Yes! And I showed her, but then she refused to take me with. Started screamin' and hollerin' about how she thinks she knows my situation. Thought I had too much in one of my bottles and said if I wanted a ride home, I'd have to count them out. Fucking bitch."

"None of that now. These are your cousin's coworkers, remember."

"Fuck, some coworkers." He threw his hands up in his lap and his voice broke. "I didn't appreciate her judging me like that so I got out."

"That all?"

"And you already know I kicked the door, fuck!"

"Hey, let's be clear. I didn't *know* any of this. Like I said, it wasn't my place. I wanted your truth before anyone else's. But rumors travel, Liam, and, I don't know, wouldn't you at least agree this is a poor showing for your community?"

"I just need a ride home so I can sleep," he said through his fingers. "No more family time, please."

"All right. Say, where about do you live in Geshig?"

"Up past Quarry Way Road. Roscoville townhouses."

"Quite a ways, 'specially now that you can't take the bus. Do you have a car?"

"Yeah, but nothing's legal on it."

"What do you mean?"

"No tabs, no insurance. Still haven't transferred the title either."

"Oh, I thought . . ." Zach paused, ready to say he'd thought Alana would've taken care of that. "Thought you didn't have your own vehicle."

"Haven't been able to use it all year, 'cept for a trip to the store here and there, but I hate to risk losing it."

A whole year? Being that far off the mark for simple paperwork seemed so ludicrous to him.

"Tell you what," Zach said. "I could pay for those for you. For now. And you could pay me back in time. Pretty patient guy. And I don't know the state of your vehicle, but if it runs, you could use it to start working again." *She looks out for him so much as is. How did Alana let him do that?* "And I'd ask you to sober up."

"Was waiting for that."

"We've all been waiting. Life's a lot of waiting."

Liam mumbled what sounded to Zach like the start of many excuses before he fell silent and then reached into his bag. He pulled up a large orange bottle, but the winter afternoon was too dark for Zach to make out what was inside.

Liam pushed the bottle back inside, zipped it, and exhaled through the nose. "Long as I'm mobile."

*

A half hour later, Liam's head bobbed up and down as the boy slept, and Zach's truck turned on Quarry Way Road, north of Geshig. Ten miles in was a trail with a green street sign that read BULLHEAD VILLAGE RD.

He reached over to shake Liam as the truck turned in, but the boy startled awake in a panic, several *what*s and *where*s on his quivering mouth.

"We're almost to yer aunt's. I dropped Alana off here earlier today. She's waiting to be picked up."

"No. No, Zach, you don't know. You have to take me home. Just home. It's miles from here."

"It's okay, I just wanted to tell Alana about the car situation. See if she's okay with it. Wouldn't wanna cross her if she's not."

Liam sobbed and shook. "No . . . just home."

Zach parked the truck outside a small green house. The engine was barely off when Liam's door opened and the imp tumbled out to the ground. From the front door, Alana and her great-aunt Elise walked onto the porch.

"Hey, babe, look who I found . . ." His words trailed off as he saw the look of anguish on her face.

"Zach, what did you do?"

Elise stared stoically at the writhing Liam, still in pain and growing louder. Alana jumped off of the porch, grabbed Zach's wrist, and pulled him away from the house into the yard.

"Why did you bring him here?" she screamed. "What is wrong with you?"

"He needed a ride. What the fuck are you getting mad about?"

"He can't be here, Zach! He can't come to this place; I told you about this!"

"What do you mean you told me about this?"

"I showed you my murals in the garage!"

Zach stared at her, dumbfounded and shocked at the hysterical words coming from the mother of his child. "You've got to be fuckin' joking, Alana. Your paintings? That's the reason?"

After a few months of dating, Alana had brought him into her art studio, where several canvases were drying and many more lined the walls. Mostly watercolor works, but some oils and acrylics. All, she claimed, were in some way portents of the future. Visions from some dream-fire in her mind.

The biggest painting was a triptych, with the inner panel an image of Elise's green house and the outer two the woods and lake that surrounded it. Above all, a silver-gold thread hung over the scene like a moon dog. A barrier.

Even in the twilight he could see her glaring daggers into his eyes. "You don't believe me. You've never respected a word I've said about my culture."

"Alana, I take everyone's belief system with a grain of salt. That's just the way of the world." Liam's moans turned to coughs and hacks. "Jesus, what is wrong with him?"

"It's the methadone, jackass! The land doesn't like it. The land doesn't like bad medicine. Which you would've known if you'd just listened to me in the first place!"

The screen door on the house slammed shut. Alana threw her hands in the air, tears running down her face. "Now I gotta go explain to Elise why one of her nephews is like this."

"Wait, she didn't know?"

She turned her back to him.

"She *didn't know?*"

"I was handling it," she said, back still turned, teeth clamped firmly together.

"There it is," Zach said. "That's what I've been saying for months, Alana. You've been coddling him and making excuses and completely unwilling to hear someone objective on this."

"You are not objective! You've hated him since the moment you met him and knew nothing about his situation!"

"Don't tell me I don't know about this stuff, Alana. I can see it every day when I walk through the casino. I could see it back at home with my family, too, so don't give me that. Anyone who wasn't his favorite cousin could see he's abusing his dosage! Even Cherie was—"

"Get out."

"Don't do this."

"Get out. Go away, Zach. Get in your truck. Leave my aunt's land, and don't call me."

She walked over to Liam, helped him to his feet, and then brought him to Elise's small sedan in the driveway. Alana put him in the passenger seat. Zach rubbed his temples with his fingertips, ready to push through this fight and help her see reason.

"Don't worry about custody," Alana said. "I'm not gonna keep our child from you, but I'll see as little of you as possible."

She peeled out of the parking lot, throwing her engagement ring out of the driver's-side window, where it landed at his feet.

Chapter 10 ☠ WOODPECKER FRENZY

GLENN NIELAN

December 20, 2017

Hᵉ'd been reviewing the footage from the hostel over and over, looking for any sign of the boy from the app, when the guard Cherie sent him a text.

Mr. Big Smiles is back if u still wanted to talk to him.

George???

Yah who else lol. Go get 'im, boy.

He sent back a row of thumbs-up and praying hands, and then he was out the cabin door. It was a heavy snowfall, but he didn't notice until his thin loafers were cold and soaked through. He was so eager to see the big man he'd rushed out into the winter without thinking about bundling up.

Half a mile up the paved trail, the trees thinned, and the glow of Atlantis gave the early evening a yellow-orange hue, the color of a scratched-up car blinker. The back parking lot of the casino was a sea of black ice hidden by white velvet. Several times he almost slipped and broke his damn skull open. At least he'd finally get an answer from the flighty patron host.

Glenn beelined to the patron services counter, where

Mr. Big Smile was shooting the breeze with a customer in a walker. He waited in line behind two more patrons before George finally acknowledged him.

"What can I do you fer, fella?"

With that, Glenn's final shred of patience melted away like the ice on his loafers. "It's been weeks, George, so I was hoping you'd have an answer for me."

"On your request?"

"Yes, on my request. What else? You said you'd deliver it to the top of the tribe's desk."

"And I did, just like I said."

"So? Have they agreed?"

"Oh, I guess the letter must've went to your listed address automatically."

"I've been up here this whole time, George. You know that."

"It's just how the technology works, eh, chap? It's effective, no doubt, but every government uses equipment from the early eighties, don'tcha know?"

"Jesus fuck, George, are they gonna grant the funding or not?"

The patron host never broke smile or composure. "They've declined your request. I'm sorry about that, friend. Better luck next time. Do you need some help with your membership card? It's points day for our seniors."

"Now listen here!" Glenn slammed his fist on the counter. Still, the host didn't jump, though everyone at the desk and in line behind him did. "You've put me off for weeks, and that's all you have to say?"

"Why don't we talk in my office, bud."

George unlatched the golden end of the velvet rope and beckoned him beyond the counter. Red rushed to Glenn's face—anger, embarrassment, both—as he walked away from the commotion he'd created.

Inside the cramped office, the host took a seat in a fading office chair, but Glenn pushed the only other chair aside and glowered over the tiny desk.

"You said this was a sure thing. You said you'd make it happen, that you'd put your word in!"

"Now, Glenn, you know I'm not a tribal member here. I have no power to make promises like that."

"But you did!"

"I did not. I told you'd I'd help pitch it and that you could count on me for that, but for final approval I never said it'd be absolute."

"Bullshit!" Glenn scrambled for his phone. "That's not what you said." While he flipped through the app screens, hoping to pull up their chained conversation, George lazily hit a few buttons on his keyboard, and the monitor pulled up a few chains of his own.

"See?" he said. "I told you I was down to help you make it happen, *for sure*. I didn't say the tribe would *approve it for sure*."

George thought he felt tears welling as he relooked at their exchanges, and sure enough, this squirrelly little fuck was right. There'd been no assurances, nothing promised, but between those lines, so much encouragement. So much certitude in tone. George had seemed just as convinced as Glenn that coming to Languille Lake for this project would ignite great interest, a flourishing of creativity and ideas. He claimed to have heard rumors in the community of film crews headed by burgeoning Indigenous voices, gung-ho ghost hunters and paranormalists looking for bigfoots, aspiring documentarians like himself, all so captivated by this lush land.

Land of lush, he thought as he looked at the crystal decanter on George's shelf next to an hourglass in a mahogany frame.

"Did they say why? Did they say anything at all?"

"I guess there were privacy and tact concerns. No one was too keen on dredging up the recent past—or the distant past, for that matter. And who could blame them? Stepping foot onto a reservation, one must prepare for a lot of lingering grief, *mon frère*. I know it's not easy news to hear, especially after you've been such a good boy about waiting. But hey, it's the casino economy for ya. Sometimes you win the reels; sometimes they spin ya right down the river."

Glenn heard the word *boy* and looked straight into his old friend's eyes.

Earlier when they'd first reconnected, he'd noted how attractive and magnetic the businessman presented himself, but Glenn thought it wasn't a deep, personal feeling of attraction. Much too old he'd become. Only this was a face he'd looked to in that way years ago, even going so far as to befriend Tiffany and her friends who knew him, just to have an excuse to talk. Back when those decisions weren't conscious and the idea so unthinkable, so unnatural—dreadful, a sure ticket to ostracization by his family and community.

The eyes of a former friend and crush stared back at him with the cold demure of a man with dollar signs tattooed on his irises.

"So. Tell ya what." George dug into his drawer, scrawled an ugly line on a colorful postcard, and handed it to Glenn. "I'll give you twenty dollars in patron points. Have yourself a good time out there, bud."

Glenn grabbed the ticket and stormed out of the office, across the maze of lights, and back out into the parking lot, with black ice below and cerulean dusk above. In the shadow of the trees, the slate-silver waves of the lake billowing between the barren shrubs, he dropped to his knees, and a scream ripped from his stomach out into the night.

A whistle in the woods, some late-traveling bird, returned his call with three short notes.

Glenn had been played for a fool, and, as always, the house had won.

*

The next night, Glenn found himself back inside Hidden Atlantis, his stack of newspapers full of dead, smiling ink faces proving again to be depressing company. He sought comfort in the checkerboard flash of keno.

The twenty dollars George had granted him quickly drained to zero credits, but he could spare a few more bills. The squeaky wheels of the refreshment cart stopped behind him.

"Need anything, high roller?" said the man behind the cart, whose name tag said DIEGO. "Cup of joe, bowl of fruit?"

"Fruit?"

"Yep. Got a tropical spread today."

Glenn grabbed the little white food tray, and sure enough, there were two small skewers of yellow and orange fruit.

"Goes great with salt, my man."

"Really?"

"Of course. Let me sprinkle a little love on you." Diego winked and pulled a glass vial of salt from his apron.

Glenn ate the fruit, the salt mixing with the moist, acidic strand, and asked if Diego could bring him a drink from the bar.

"What's your poison tonight, Glenn?"

"One Mermaid Castle." He pulled his phone from his

pocket, the grid of faces waiting for him to turn on his charming fingers and dig in.

"Sure. Why not?" Diego said with a chuckle. "A Mermaid for the gentleman. And you should probably take a cold shower, guy. I can see you scoping me." Diego winked, and the cart disappeared into the labyrinthine screens.

Sixty dollars down, Glenn was sick of the number grid and left the keno section. Three rows down he found an old machine, one still with a working lever. A vestigial crank from another era. Faded red letters spelled out WOODPECKER FRENZY III: SAP SUCKER MANIA! with a generic cartoon woodpecker perched on the F.

Glenn sipped the rest of his Mermaid Castle and sat down. He played the max bet, max lines, and with tap after tap of the hard plastic buttons, cartoon woodpeckers, sunsets, leaves, and the usual cherries and 7s reeled past his face.

"Another, Diego. This time add scotch."

The server had another drink in Glenn's hand a moment later. He hadn't even heard the wheels of his fruit cart over the slot machine's sound effects, which he always set to max to drown out the other slot machine zombies.

"One more."

"Is two okay?" Diego said. "Just the whiskey now."

Glenn tipped the man a one-hundred-dollar bill. "You read my mind, honey."

"Have fun, bud."

Three spins later, five woodpeckers aligned on the screen and triggered a bonus of fifty free games. He took another sip of whiskey, and when he looked down from the glass, only ten spins out of the fifty were left.

Next to him, a fellow gambler pounded the screen with the side of his hand. "C'mon!" he screamed.

Glenn rubbed at the bruise in the middle of his forehead after he pulled his head from the glass.

"Careful now," Diego said, gripping Glenn on the shoulders. "If you fall asleep, we'll have to kick you out. And we'd never want our high rollers to stop playing."

Glenn sputtered out a weak, "Huh?" before feeling his eyelids droop, knowing he had no way to stop himself from slamming into the screen again.

The lights flickered out, leaving only a blue text box with SERVICE NEEDED in flashing white words.

*

When he opened his eyes, he saw a glossy white slip of paper inches from his face, held by the steady hand of George. He was back in George's office, where all sides of the man's desk were swarming in paperwork, most in plastic-wrapped boxes but others strewn about in piles, and anything not wrapped or crumpled up was at the mercy of the draft from the ceiling fan above.

"Didn't we settle this before, George?"

"We hope you enjoy your stay at Hidden Atlantis."

Before he could respond, Glenn heard a steady mechanical tap coming from the desk. An invisible hand, tapping out words as George held a vacant smile and didn't move the coupon out of Glenn's face.

A door slammed. The desk lamp flickered, and he was back at *Woodpecker Frenzy*, still waiting for service. Four empty whiskey glasses sat on the slot machine's front panel, waiting for the drink boy with the cart to come around and collect.

*

In the dream, it had been days of no food and no sex, and the hunger grew so intense he'd agreed to host a Zeus instead of an Adonis. The white-bearded man had grabbed Glenn's shoulders, shoved him to the bed, and wrapped his legs around his furry neck.

"Are you ready for the power of Olympus?"

Da-da-da da-da daaa daa!

Across the screen, another bonus animation played. A toga-clad Zeus hurling lightning bolts toward the reels at random, each square hit shocked and transformed into more credits for the win. The machine's label read ZEUS LANDING.

"That is one hot bank of machines," Diego said as he walked by. On all sides, other patrons were enjoying the same game as he. A big-chested god on a mountain hurling pixelated dollars into their coffers.

Glenn rubbed at his temples and sighed. "He's not even my type . . ."

"Didn't look like it from this angle."

To his left, the boy from the first day. The delicate fairy boy who was so light on his feet and quick with a smile.

"Do I need to teach you how to play again?" Puck pointed with his lips beyond their current bank of *Zeus Landing*. "It's all games of chance, my bear. Random number generators. Robbing good fellas like you is what it does. You never needed to leave *Cleopatra's Coins* for that thrill."

*

He intended to stand up and look for a machine attendant so he could get back to his free games, but after he rubbed the sleep from his eyes, his reflection in his own computer screen stared back. By instinct, he moved the mouse, and it flickered back on instantly.

A cold draft from the cabin's thin birchbark walls brushed across his toes. He was back in his cabin, in the woods behind the casino.

On the screen his camera footage showed the entrance to the slide at the water park. Glenn couldn't see any lifeguards or kids in the background, just blurry shades of pale-blue-and-white pool tiles. For a moment, the camera's angle showed his face, in the midst of him attaching it to an innertube. It must have been his waterproof action camera.

Seconds later, the innertube jerked forward, and the footage descended into the maw of the slide. He froze, felt his heart slow but his breath quicken, and he didn't want to hit pause but somehow knew he'd find his hand on the mouse at the right moment and see her.

Tiffany . . . why didn't you stay away?

He clicked the mouse, but instead of the thin sheet of plastic, it was, once again, the hard square of plastic with the words *Max Bet* underneath. He looked up and saw the oasis motifs, the river, the golden idols of the sand, and dark-haired women in sparse linens.

It was *Grandeur of the Nile* after all, wasn't it?

Diego's cart rounded the corner of the banks, and he tossed him a bottle of Gatorade. "Stay hydrated, my dog."

"Thanks, man." Glenn fumbled with the seal before taking a long, sugary gulp. "Do you have the time?"

Diego looked up and around at the building's walls, then at his empty wrist, and then shrugged. "Few do these days."

Glenn stood up and took his phone out of his pocket. Low battery, and the poor reception in the building had prevented the internal clock from giving a proper reading. There was no way it could still be evening.

In the lounge between the hotel and the casino floor, Glenn plugged in his phone and took a short nap while it charged. When he looked up, the phone had charged up to 35 percent. The lockscreen showed his dating app inbox had several bites from prospective pups.

He opened the phone, and instead of the hungry grid of men, it was camera footage from the camera he'd hidden in the ceiling of his hotel room. Glenn's heart rate sped up. He was watching the encounter with the first young man he'd hosted. The lover had insisted on darkness out of fear and privacy. Glenn had obliged and left the lights off.

He scrambled to light a cigarette. Somehow, he knew it would be of no relief to the nervous man to know that in night vision footage, no one would recognize his face or his body or what Glenn did to both.

Da-da-da da-da daaa daa!

On-screen, the woodpeckers drilled at birch trees until circular sections peeled away and revealed hidden credits etched into the inner bark. Eventually, there were enough credits to trigger the mega-jackpot advertised at the top tier.

"Congratulations, sir!"

Glenn stared at the pile of hundred-dollar bills the attendant counted into his palms. The amount looked substantial, but he didn't remember how much the employee had told him it was. He also had a hard time finding joy when he could see at his feet dozens of ATM withdrawal slips.

"I think I need a smoke break."

Diego tossed him a book of matches from the cart. "Life without a smoke break, haunted house without a heartache."

In the atrium of Atlantis, Glenn struggled to light the

cigarette in the wind, but he managed after hiding behind one of the plaster columns. Snow fell from heavy gray clouds, and he still had no idea what time it was.

*

His socks in his flip-flops had soaked through from the storm, which had dropped just over an inch of snow by the time he reached the cabin. Inside, he took a long shower, first cold to acclimate his feet, then gradually hot and scalding. The temperature helped take his mind off his bank account, something he would check by the end of the day, but not quite yet. After a whole night of gambling, he wasn't in the mood for bookkeeping.

Glenn sat at his computer desk in a thin white bathrobe. A circus melody of bells played from his speakers. An illicit video of the pharaoh slot machine, one he knew the casino would frown on, played as the bonus game was once again triggered.

He tapped the keyboard, and the next video played. As soon as he saw this second young man who walked in, the memory of their app exchange came back.

His profile name was RuggedBoi. Unlike the previous shadow lover, this one had no shame about a profile with his face, abs, and ass as his available selection. Glenn remembered their courtship being short and to the point.

What are you looking for, cutie?

A man who can keep up with me.

What a coincidence. I'm looking for a boy to obey me and let me tie him and have my way with him.

LOL ok. But I gotta know the safe word.

I'll tell you before we start, promise. ;)

Click after click, video after video, a small parade of young lovers floated across the threshold and rolled with him all over the eiderdown. With each video, patches of small brown burn holes spread across the fabric.

One met him late, late into the evening, undeterred by the snow, confident his lifted truck would prevail. When this blond Adonis walked on screen, Glenn's face on the bed was hungry, gaunt even. Big bags under his eyes.

Glenn cringed as he heard himself growl through the computer speakers.

"Can I ask you something . . . ?"

"Anything, daddy," the Adonis said as he lay on the bed and shed his clothes, his yellow jersey already damp with sweat on the shoulders and lower back.

"Will you let me teach you to be a good boy?"

The young man laughed when he saw the blue vinyl dog mask in Glenn's hand. "Oh. Wow. Um . . ." The boy put on the mask. "It's . . . well, this is just . . . woof."

He grabbed the boy's chin and pulled him close.

You don't feel real, but you do feel soft.

*

Once again, an alarm woke him, but this time it sent him into a small fit of shakes and gasps.

A loud siren assaulted his ears as a group of cartoon cows in red hats slid down a fire pole. On the top screen, a cow in a stable kicked glass lanterns to the bottom screen, where they landed on reel squares and the resulting fire revealed bonus credits.

Glenn looked to his left and right, but there were no other customers. Must be a turtle Tuesday. He stood up, tipped the chair against the screen as the bonus game feature played on, and drifted his way to the men's room. Luckily, there was no one inside.

He took three orange pills from a folded five-dollar bill in the left lower pocket of his cargo shorts. Three was probably too many, but anything to stay awake.

An old man in a blue peasant shirt walked out of a stall just as Glenn popped the pills. He blushed. "I'm so sorry."

The other man held up two hands. "Secret's safe with me, guy. This is the only place they can't see that, ya know." He gestured upward with his index fingers.

Something about his smile bothered Glenn.

"Is that true?"

"Of course. But I suppose you'd be paranoid about that, wouldn't you?"

"Excuse me?"

The man's smile widened, revealing two crooked front teeth like a rat. "Live, laugh, panopticon."

Glenn washed his hands and left the old man behind in the bathroom.

*

A bird's whistle woke him. His phone's grating notification sound.

When he opened the app, the message was from the boy who he'd just been dreaming of.

Dream of an angel, and he shall appear . . .
Puck?
Hey its you! the boy replied. *Never got to see you that night. :)*
Yeah. It's been a very long month... :(
Oh hunny Why u sad?

Sigh . . . ya know, it's just sometimes things don't work out.

Like the day we met. ;)

Exactly. But some long term plans I had didn't go my way. So I'm finding myself with a lot of free time.

Ya don't say... :)

What you thinking, hot stuff?

I don't got much going on, myself, Puck replied. *I can come see you.*

I'd like that. You look close, you at the casino? I'm in Cabin 26.

Ok. I'll be there shortly, Glenjamin. ;P

Wait! I have to ask you something first!!

A network error scrambled the bars on his phone, and it took a few extra seconds to send, but by then the boy's icon had gone offline.

He paced back and forth, checking the blinds every minute or so, hoping he hadn't imagined it or that this wasn't some asshole catfish or flake.

But sure enough, a dark shape in the pale blue woods bounded up to his door. Glenn opened it, and the same boy from the pool greeted him with an impish smile.

"Hey there, ol' man. Heard you were looking to give a dog a bone."

"Hi there, stranger . . . listen, about that."

Before he could warn him, Puck fluttered past him and into the open space of the cabin, eyes instantly fixed on a tray on the table with a white-dappled cast-iron kettle filled with long strands of sugar.

"I tried to tell you before you came. I didn't know maple sugar burned so easily."

"Ohh . . ." Puck whispered, crossing a lithe arm over his stomach and bringing a high-bent hand to his chin. "You didn't lie. You really are from the rez."

His nerves broke with the sound of the boy's laughter and he heaved a deep growl of relief before joining him.

"Like I said, it's been a rough month."

Then the boy let Glenn kiss him with a mouthful of the sweet, spun sugar, strands so light and ghostly that Puck's lips shivered, the taste of his wintergreen skoal pack attacking his lover's mouth like an icy wind.

The chemical mix broke Puck's laugh into a squeaky cough. "The moon's only at a quarter, and we're partying like it's full."

"You don't have to stay here with all this garbage. You should head home."

"Oh, please. I've seen worse. I've even done worse," Puck said. "I'm more interested in this." He floated over to Glenn's bed and pawed at the ropes, the clamps, the harnesses and suits, and, finally, the mask. He picked it up and scratched at the black spandex nose. "Oh, you like pretending to be *animosh*."

"Not just any animal. A dog. But not me. You."

"*Animosh* means dog in Ojibwe, *chimookoman*. Aw, and here I already said you were from the rez." Puck tilted his head and looked at Glenn from the corners of his eyes, his smile a serpent crawling across his face. "There's nothing in this mask for me."

"It's okay."

"Not to shame, of course. Just saying." The boy winked and gave an audible click with his inner cheek and teeth. "Indians don't need masks to feed their animal spirit."

Puck put the mask down, and his attention turned to the wastebasket in the corner of the room under a table. "Oh."

Glenn winced as he remembered the bag full of discarded Trojan wrappers. "What a big appetite for men you have."

"Don't we all."

He tried to embrace the boy from behind, but he turned around quick, nearly taking out Glenn's nose with his chin. But he didn't stop him when he leaned in for a kiss.

"No," he said as he pulled away, though he thought Puck lingered. "Your mouth is way too innocent for me. You'd better run from here."

Puck reached up and tousled his short, thinning hair. "Another night. Or day. I'm still down for the lazy river if you are."

Glenn watched him waltz to the door, sad, but ready to beckon another caller on his phone, one he'd feel less guilty about corrupting. But then the boy turned back at the threshold of the door, a smile full of thin, sharp teeth, not yet dulled by time and use.

"Can I give you some advice I gave an old Indian once?"

Glenn chuckled. "Sure."

"Every day they don't eat, you'll have more power over them."

He watched the empty space with slow breath until the snow outside surely had covered the boy's tracks, and it was back to apps to hunt for another man.

*

What he found was a pup, and two more followed soon after.

The first was a young Native man with braided hair who refused to take off his dog mask once he walked in the door.

"What's your name, boy?"

"Noodles."

"You can call me Brutus."

"Okay."

Glenn grabbed him by the chin. "Okay, what?"

"Okay, Brutus."

"I need you to do something for me. To prove that you'll really be mine."

Moments later, Noodles crawled out of the cabin door, down the icy porch steps, as Glenn followed behind. He made the boy crawl through the snow forty yards until they reached the shore.

"The moon is full tonight." Glenn unhooked the leash and pushed the boy into the icy water. "Howl."

His voice echoed across the glossy lake and dark blue sky. "More." The boy obliged until his voice was crackly and shivering. "Time for your treat."

The boy crawled out of the water and scrambled quickly back up the snow-covered shore.

The echoing rattle of a woodpecker cut across the night.

"Are you home early, younger brother?" Glenn said. "Or did your family abandon you?" The bird rattled on in response. "Answer him, pup."

The man on the leash obeyed, sending a deep voice echoing into the woods, though way to human.

"Rough, boy. *Ruff.*"

A deep growl exploded from the vinyl mask. Glenn dropped the leash. He and his companion sprinted away from the cabin, away from the lakeshore. No words between them, no more illusion of control.

Both were in black winter under a grove of thick birchbark trees. Sharp chirps and deep knocks greeted them in all directions. When the chorus faded, a ghostly orange light ran through the veins of the evergreen bark. Silver snow fell upon the grove, now taking a warm, candlelight hue, beneath the bitter gray clouds above.

Red-streaked feathers adorned the woodpecker as it waited for Glenn's and the pup's hungry bodies.

"My friends have an itch," the woodpecker said. "Will you help me heal their agony?"

Glenn grabbed a stone near the base of the tree and hacked at the hole the woodpecker had started. Then he took hold of the tree's membranous bark and slowly peeled it away. Rough strips at first, but eventually the soft tan skin underneath was exposed to the snow.

A slate-black nail, likely driven in by a power tool, lay waiting. Glenn pried the nail out of the tree. Dark birch sap flowed.

Glenn and his pup fell to their knees, and each took small strips of the sap-covered birch skin and put them into their mouths, the fibrous taste driving quick aches into their teeth.

Sweet as birch beer. Sacred and sweet.

*

Da-da-da da-da daaa daa!

And there he was, back at *Woodpecker Frenzy III: Sap Sucker Mania!*

"One last old-fashioned, big guy."

Diego handed him a glass, the dark red syrup mixing with the bourbon, three whole cherries on top and bits of muddled red flesh floating in between the ice cubes. "But that's your last one, and then you're cut off, *mon frère*."

Glenn held the glass in his hand, felt the cold drops of condensation fall over his fingertips, followed by syrup as his arm twitched and some of the syrup spilled.

On the screen, the video from the cabin. Him and another dog-masked Adonis, this one tall and adorned with neat trails of black hair over his chest, neck, and upper back. The scene and shape of canine consummation. The man whimpered and barked as Glenn howled from behind him.

To his left and right, the same video feed was on all his fellow patrons' screens.

Chapter 11 ☠ GAME OF CHANCE

ALANA BULLHEAD

December 27, 2017

Alana brought two orders of food from the restaurant to the hotel, and the steam from the top of the boxes filled the elevator with the scent of roasted lamb and cucumber sauce.

Liam had a room on the fifth floor, courtesy of the diabetes clinic where his mother worked. They'd held a game of bingo for prizes, and she'd walked away with two rooms for two nights.

"You can have my tomatoes."

She brushed the small red cubes from her gyro to his plate and flipped through the channels on the TV, the buttons slowly accumulating a greasy layer of cucumber sauce from her fingertips.

"Is Geri still on the floor?" she asked.

"I think so. Haven't heard anything in her room, and she hasn't texted."

"Do you wanna go and find her after a while?"

"Maybe. Is Zach working?"

"Oh, never mind about him, that's nothing to worry about."

"You sure, cuz? I don't know about that one, always struck me as super vindictive and mean."

"Hey, he might've turned the guards against me, but they all know this is *my* house."

As she flipped through the movies, Liam grabbed a handful of ibuprofens and took them with a glass of fountain cola. Then he took two five-milligram tablets of melatonin.

It'd only been a week since Aunt Elise had found out about Liam's state. He'd been so doped up on methadone and gabapentin—and whatever things he could find on his own that Alana had never asked about—that cutting back in this last week made him nod off worse than before.

All medicine to help him kick the worse habits, but all of it poison to her family's ancestral land. All chemicals that were not the sacred herbs of their culture's past, just another poison not meant for human skin. He would not be welcome back at Bullhead Village until he had it all under control.

The hunt for the sandman would have to wait, even though Liam objected.

"How do you think he got so powerful?" he asked with a yawn.

"By feeding," she said, settling on an old sitcom their grandmothers would've liked. "I looked at my paintings again, and I think I see him in one. His aura looks like some kind of mutant leech."

"Then why are we here?" he mumbled. "If it's not safe."

"Well, of course it's not safe, silly, but we still have to work. And he can't stop us from enjoying a night on the reels."

As soon as she heard him snore, she finished the sandwich and then left him in the room, the TV tuned to an aquarium with light piano music.

*

At the stud poker machine section, Alana found her aunt Geri in a bonus round on *Poker Cassanova*. Fifty free hands played one right after another, and by the end she'd won $330.

"Finally!" she said. "First time I've won something here in months. Did you know that your other casinos pay out better?"

"It's all the same, auntie."

"Yeah, you all say that."

"All the same."

"How's my boy?"

"Sleeping."

"Good. I told that girl of his she can't come around anymore. I bet that's where he was getting the extra doses from."

"Heh, funny. Zach and Cherie both thought so too."

"How's the baby doing, by the way?"

"Good."

"Not great to be around all the smoke," Geri said as she lit another Marlboro short.

"You know the rules. No lecturing an Indian about their tobacco."

"Ehh, get the fuck outta here, girl."

They traded laughs and watched each other's poker hands flip, the cards on the old screens so boxy and flat. For a moment, Alana forgot about the sandman.

A flash of gray and yellow passed by her three times before she noticed it was Zach. Rather than confront him or wait for his toxic suffocating to abate, she told Geri she was going for a drive to get some air.

The moment she passed through the doors and the thick

walls of Atlantis no longer blocked the signal, her phone buzzed with a single message.

Alana, it's Marion. The sandman wants to eat Geshig's guardian.

Alana stared at the screen in complete confusion.

How did Marion know about the guardian?

When she replied, the message came back undeliverable.

*

She drove the twenty miles north to Geshig in the middle of the afternoon. The painted silo sat silent next to a field by the elementary school, its two gardens hidden by deep blankets of snow.

In Geshig elementary school, children whispered about the secret lectures meant only for the ears of the Drum & Dance kids. In one telling, all the Native kids got to learn how to curse their white peers. In another iteration, the Ojibwe students learned the food at lunch was the flesh of their enemies to absorb their strength.

In Alana's experience, the Drum & Dance kids learned how to drum on a pow-wow drum and how to dance in their chosen pow-wow style. There were no secret lectures, nothing sinister, nor was the club exclusive to the Indigenous students.

But as Alana stared at the derelict, boarded-up old rice silo, she thought maybe she remembered it just a little different. A dance class, all the jingle dress and shawl girls, hand in hand around the silo, while a woman with a hand drum sang a song. Only her beat was irregular, and her singing was not vocables but actual Ojibwe words, verse, and she could understand.

Every town keeps sacred a silent guardian.
Every town keeps a sacred, silent guardian.
Every town keeps the spirit of the guardian alive.
Every town feeds the sacred, hungry guardian.

Alana's feet sank into the deep snow as she circled to the north side of the silo, where a plank of wood that had kept the door nailed shut all these years hung loose, the door itself smashed in.

She put her hands on her stomach, feeling the warmth and strength of her future son, the comfort helping her tamp down the growing fear.

Inside the silo, her feet sank into soft soil, and hundreds of strands of spider silk touched her face. She flailed her arms above her to clear them away, and when she was satisfied that enough were brushed off her gloves, she pulled out her phone and turned on the flashlight.

Beneath her feet, musty soil layered with crunching carapaces and dead insects. All around the hexagonal wooden walls of the silo were spider webs, egg sacks, and faded bundles of silk where egg sacks once were.

Death, and some arachnid life, but no sacred, silent guardian. No trace, no presence.

A silhouette blocked out the blue winter light from the door frame. Alana turned her phone light toward the door and saw the saggy hand of the sandman gripped tightly on the wood.

"Tsk, tsk, just as I thought. You came running so easily. A fish to bait, as it were. Good girl, aren't you? Don't worry. You'll win a bonus game someday. Hope springs eternal, and the slot machine reels spin forever."

As if on a spoke, he pushed the wood, and sure enough,

it spun under his grip, even the dirt beneath her feet. A searing pain struck her back as the force knocked her against the silo walls. Her whole body tumbled back and forth, up and down, her wrists, ankles, collarbones, nose, chin all colliding and smashing against the hard angles of the structure's interior.

In spite of the pain, she reached for the light, and the moment her palm caught the frame, she pulled as hard as she could. One moment later, she felt her body launch through the small door, her shoulders scraping hard against the wood as she passed.

She landed face-first in a pile of knee-high snow, the sudden icy cold a welcome, numbing shock to her battered body. When she mustered the strength to pull herself back up, the sandman was nowhere to be found, no other footprints or marks in the snow but hers.

The silo sat firmly in place, the same plank of wood across the smashed-in door, no sign of forced movement. Upon standing, she patted down her body, feeling for any sign of bruising, bleeding, or even clothing damage, but there was no pain.

She got back in her car and drove south.

*

Back at Hidden Atlantis, she attempted to walk through the front doors without notice from Zach, but he was waiting for her outside.

"I don't wanna hear it, Zach. I'm not here for you."

As she approached the entrance and his face came into view under the canopy lights, she froze as the vermillion veins bulged in his tear-soaked eyes.

She didn't hear him say that Cherie had overdosed. She couldn't have heard that because that wasn't a world that made sense to her, but for some reason, she collapsed into her ex-fiancé's arms anyway.

A Sandman Triumphant

There's a truth about this town, one that every single citizen will learn. None will remember or know when it happened, but they've been alone on some night when no other ships were around and *I* passed by.

Tranquil skies, white-capped waves in the wind, black ice across the highway, toppled trees in a summer storm. None hold back destiny. Few possess the power to dominate destiny itself, and that's why I ate destiny's eternal heart. It beats now, somewhere tucked under my skin, a wheezing alarm clock consumed and reshaped like a shriveling placenta.

They will never feel it, never suspect my hands running through their veins, but I am the weight that holds them in place, the stringer that keeps the walleye in the shoal enough to breathe but not escape. Every black plastic eye in the sky, every ceiling tile bearing those false retinas, every doorway, every window, the ugly metal top of the telephone poles, the mourning gray of the sky, the dancing shadows of the woods, the currents of chemical electricity in their blood, all flow from my design.

Where I stand now, high above my golden palace of victory, my clockwork ghosts below, they bet, they spend, they nod. Most of all, they nod, and every convulsion that saves their faces from breaking the glass of their machines, my sweet kiss.

Man can suffer from too much sleep.

Chapter 12 ♣ THE GHOST DANCE MACABRE

DIEGO MOOSE

December 31, 2017

Thy soul shall find itself alone
'Mid dark thoughts of the gray tombstone—
Not one, of all the crowd, to pry
Into thine hour of secrecy.

Be silent in that solitude,
Which is not loneliness—for then
The spirits of the dead who stood
In life before thee are again
In death around thee—and their will
Shall overshadow thee: be still.

—EDGAR ALLAN POE

Underneath a blanket of ghost-stale air, the Hidden Atlantis poker lounge held their weekly Texas Hold 'Em tournament. Registration started at five and ended after midnight, the first few minutes of December 31.

With a full house, starting with Jacks in hand, Diego had won the tournament and claimed just shy of $1,190. He attributed it to beginner's luck, even though by then he'd lived a few more years of play at the casino than years in childhood.

In the past twenty years of third-hill gambling, he'd stuck to games of chance, with only the occasional dip into the cards.

Diego looked at his fallen competitors, who were generally more boisterous types, and felt just a little pity. Beginner's luck *could* explain it, but then, their usual smiles and cajoling were dampened and soft in the wake of the showdown, their loss to his Jacks full of deuces. Not the seething, silent anger that hard men carried, but a quiet humility, calm minds with slow, glossy eyes.

I hope these gentle friends haven't run afoul of my sandman.

He left the table with a small bucket full of chips. None of the men said *cheater,* and the eagles above certainly never would either, but he could feel it welling so hard it finally echoed, all their voices at once, in his skull. He could hear them in fits of coughs and deep laughs, joyous even in financial ruin and ritual defeat.

Never play against the house, eh, Wovoka?

Those decades ago, it was his brother Wovoka who had first brought the younger Diego through the casino doors and led him through the rows with sharp eyes, intent on showing him a proper tour across the sea, where the best boons and battles worth fighting were to be found, and had even treated him to a few free nights of bingo.

But those days were as long gone as the foundation where that casino stood. Holdover from the world their mother, Igra, grew up in, where the slow growth of the tribal gaming interests were in the limbo of bureaucracy, of treaties old and new, and from it all, a bloom of opulence, a step to bring in the end of a century, and the dawn of the casino economy. The old community bingo center in Waubajeeg where Igra spent endless hours—and piles of old purple-and-gold daubers— with her sisters, cousins, and childhood friends grown into mothers and grandmothers. Not just there, but others across the state. Magic Midnight in Kildere. Haley's Comet way over in Turkey Feather. The bar Sweetie's Cabin on the shores of Half Lake, where bags full of discarded bingo cards and pull tabs were cast into the dumpsters in heavy, compacted bricks wound with hard plastic ties.

Haven't played bingo in so long, brother. Old games seldom die, but maybe if enough people fall, so will our mother's second-favorite casino game.

Diego cashed out his chips, leaving a crisp hundred-dollar bill in the hands of a chipper cashier, and then left Hidden Atlantis on foot, east on the Keno Road, though he hadn't played that game since last month. Nor would he play any games until the new year.

Tonight would be all hands on deck at Hidden Atlantis. A $2,018 prize awaited some hopeful spirit, and the management expected a big crowd.

He walked toward Indian Hollow, casting one cigarette in the ditch for each two smoked.

*

Wovoka had encouraged him to stay at his first job at eighteen, even when he came home the first week in a huff, half-tears, complaining about what bullshit the casino was, what a bullshit soul-suck working was, what a bullshit world it was outside their cracker-box rez housing.

His older brother poured him a shot of whiskey.

"Sounds like you finally learned why people drink."

"I don't want to." Diego turned red as he remembered growling the brattish line through his gritted teeth. "I'm not that kind of Indian."

"You're no better or worse than that kind of Indian," Wovoka said. "But you deserve it because you're a working Indian now."

Diego threw back the whiskey, and Wovoka laughed when he had to help him to the sink so he could cough, get a drink of water, and then wobble back to the kitchen table, where the glass was already filled again.

"Your first one hurts, doesn't it? Work is like that. It'll leave a bad taste on your tongue until you get used to it. Then you might even start to like it. And what's not to like, brother? A casino is for fun. The shifts are long, but it's only a little bit of work. Just a little bit of long work, eh?"

He laughed and wiped his tears, and the anger receded. So hard to recall nearly two decades back, but he knew the anger had receded. Back in the days when Wovoka could actually do that for him.

Little bit of long work, Diego thought as he pushed his fruit-and-drink cart around. *That's how the reservation clock works.*

It took two decades of bouncing from job to job, casino to casino, rez to rez—and so many land acknowledgments—for Diego to end up back home where their mother, Igra, raised him and Wovoka, serving refreshments and goodies to his people.

"For my favorite gal," he said to Jenny Hunter, an elderly white woman with curly spider-silk hair and a gaudy coat of faux fur.

"Oh you," she said, accepting the little cup of tropical fruits and a Styrofoam of coffee. "Better be turning these machines up."

He feigned the polite, high-society laugh he'd learned in poker dens in few different Indian casinos that happened to be near big cities. "Oh, they'd never let me get near them." He winked at her as she took a bite of orange papaya. "I'm not responsible enough for such power."

"Nonsense, hun. I see you in here almost every day. Ol' reliable you'll be one day. I know."

"Right back at you, Ms. Jenny. Wouldn't have it any other way. Oh, by the way, where's your daughter? I thought she had Saturdays off."

"She does, but my grandbaby has a recital today. I'm here by myself."

"Okay, well, you call me if you need anything. My phone's on."

He pressed on to more rows with his boxes of fruit, ice, pitchers of coffee and soda, with an apron full of matches, wet naps for coin dust, seashell pens clipped to all his pockets, and a fanny pack with a small bank for guests who needed change or a top-off on nickel rolls.

These days, people asked for the coin less and less, but there were still stalwarts like Ms. Jenny who resisted technological change and preferred a coin slot and a crank while she waited for wins. Seven years previously, when he was first offered this fruit boy role, he'd been tempted to reject it when they required him to carry a change bank. Bitter then, and bitter now, the memory of a job handling currency in Milwaukee ate at him. Innocent as he knew he was, in the end there was no fighting the numbers, and he was left with a three-hundred-dollar debt to the casino, which then fired him, keeping his last paycheck to cover their loss.

Since then, he was not keen on cash. But he was keen on people. He took the job with pride—dedicated himself to it, really—and the tips in the years since more than made up for that bad choice and worse luck suffered seven years ago.

One day, I'll go back to Milwaukee. Soon as I walk in a guest, they'll be lining up to rub the bulge in my pants and beg me to bless them with whatever spills out.

One day.

On his route, near the east end of the floor, two young women stood near the water park entrance. They looked no older than fifteen, both nervous, withdrawn, leaning into each other while whispering and looking his direction.

"Can I help you girls? Gotta stay in the park area or the hotel."

They weren't over the line just yet, but all employees were encouraged to be on the lookout for lost youths of the land.

"We want some quarters for the arcade, but the machine is broken and we don't know where to go."

"Oh, that's no problem, girls," he said, trying his best to sound gentle and friendly. "I have some quarters on me."

They handed him a five-dollar bill, and from his bank he ripped open a ten-dollar roll and counted out twenty quarters for the girls.

"Oh, fer pretty," one of the girls said. "This one is painted." She held up a quarter with a glossy red coating.

"Oh, would you look at that."

"I wanna keep this one. Can I get more?" the older of the two said, handing him a crumpled dollar bill that was thinner than tissue.

"Whatever you'd like. Now you better get back into the arcade, or I'll get some funny looks from the guards." He winked, and the girls scurried back inside, giggling and screaming.

He turned his cart back to the maze of lights, bringing his services wherever needed. Soda, coffee, fruit baskets. Matchbooks, stir sticks. Paper cups coated in wax, Styrofoam cups, stir sticks, sugar, sweetener, all with a smile.

Drink up, my somnambule gamblers. There is plenty of my syrup for all.

With the hard plastic pitchers of soft drinks depleted, Diego rolled the cart into a small hallway near the western quadrant that led to the viscous beating heart of the beverage operation. In a large, cooled room near the kitchen were all the kegs and soft drink syrups. Black plastic valves and opaque tubes distributed the soda to the casino's seemingly endless stations of free fountain calories. Dingy metal taps on silver kegs, the hoses a mess of strands like an ambitious yellow fungus.

This rat king of taps, so perfect for a nation so entwined in syrup. Lab made or tree, drink to me, all my sweet cousins.

Diego did a quick check of the syrups and kegs before he brought his cart of empty pitchers to the only back-of-house drink fountain.

The cold, crisp sound of carbonation gushed into his pitchers, an overflowing mop of bubbles on each spout. Brown cola trickled over his knuckles.

The cleansing burn of the bubbles, that sticky feeling of regret. What a sweat lodge awaits those who can't step away from this temple of sacred spigots.

A fair few nights of the year, the casino was too crowded for his cart, so he walked through the throng with a silver tub of drinks attached to his shoulders with a pair of black suspenders. His shift officially ended at eleven, but eventually his supervisor noted how difficult navigation inside the casino had become and dismissed him at ten thirty.

He smoked four cigarettes in the parking lot after he clocked out, doubled back around the front of the casino, and walked in as a guest.

On New Year's Eve, most were only there for the drawing, and it was almost impossible to find an open machine. Instead, he found himself in the observer's corner behind the blackjack tables. All the dealers wore those silly holiday glasses and hats that said 2018.

The same amount would be given to ten lucky patrons at the last minute of midnight, but as an employee, he couldn't enter his name. He only wanted to observe the frenzy as the names called, if present, exploded with excitement and attempted to make their way through the crowd now poised to scream as the New Year second passed.

"2018," he whispered as he watched the dealers fan the deck on the table. *Two whole decades since you were here, dear Igra. So much has changed in such a short time.*

His mother had been a part-time blackjack dealer from the days of the Waubajeeg Community Bingo's first inception, when it was little more than a warehouse with a basic short-order kitchen. Her other job was an office aide in the tribal legal department, where her days were boring but calm and stable compared to the nights that the casino brought for her.

Wovoka, this is true heritage. The green velvet, the plastic chips. Love for the ages. Didn't her light shine so bright? Hers and her old man's, Greg. Et lux perpetua.

In the early eighties, Igra Moose had met her future husband when he lost seven hundred dollars at her table. Gregory had been hitting on her throughout the night, tipping generously, and by the time the last call at the bar came, he'd taken a Sharpie and written his number on the chip that last fell into her tip box.

They wouldn't connect for months because she'd refused

to collect the number from the chip, something he would playfully hold over her head in front of his family and friends every now and then. They connected in the break room; some casino patrons told him when they recognized who their beverage server was.

"Oh, Igra was the nicest woman. Shame about Gregory, hun," said one older woman, rubbing his wrist when he handed her a paper cup of diet cola.

"Oh, Igra was such a card. No one could outdrink her without her permission, heh."

"Oh, Igra, the poor dear. I know she never wanted kids, but Gregory insisted."

Diego found ways over the years to listen to the casino chatter, whispers, and gossip to piece together stories of their parents he knew his brother, Wovoka, had never known. Springtime stories from stiff-legged elders who'd known either Igra or Gregory from infancy. Both were loud, fussy babies, screaming for days and days on end, as if they had something pertinent to say from some past life. Such spirited babes could only grow into determined adults, seeking what they'd learn too late was only veneer, the ebb and flow of human misery in tobacco-stained halls.

Wintry stories of a doe-eyed couple trying to partake in that most primal game of chance.

Igra fell in love with Gregory quickly, and Gregory knew it, convincing her early on to wed and start a family. The perfect match, two of the old bloods from Pillager days, both Languille Lake enrollees. So much made sense in their whirlwind love.

Mother couldn't tell him, Wovoka. He never knew she didn't want us.

Gregory Moose convinced her to adopt two wayward Native boys who'd been bouncing through the foster system for over a year: Wovoka five, Diego not yet two. And one day, they might have kids of their own, if the Creator blessed them.

Later, when Diego was thirteen, Igra told him something he knew wouldn't have come were it not for a bottle of wine, one much stronger than what she was used to.

"I think your father was sterile. I don't think he could've ever had his own children."

She passed out and never spoke of it again, dear Wovoka.

A snowmobile accident had taken Gregory on an early trip to the Fourth Hill of Winter, and Igra was stuck with two adopted boys, whom she never truly wanted in the first place, and a heart so pained she never stepped foot in a casino again.

Hey, Wovoka, is that why she stopped talking to you?

Diego caught a flash of black hair and royal-purple sequins. A woman he recognized.

"Hey, Jess! Wait up!" Diego shuffled away from the crowd, afraid he'd lose track of Ms. Jenny's daughter.

"Oh! Diego, hi!"

Jess turned back and threaded her way to him through the crowd, spreading her arms for a hug.

"Must be here for the drawing?" she said.

"Oh, no. Employees can't enter."

"Oh, that's too bad. Guess I'm glad I got out of here," she said with an awkward laugh.

"Oh, yeah. You're working, right? Your mom said something about you having Saturdays off."

"Yeah, I've been at the Bertram County office. So far, so good. So white, though."

"Ha. I bet. Hey, is Ms. Jenny here?"

"She's around. I was just about to go find her, actually. Do you wanna come with?"

"Nah, I better get going soon. But give my best to your mother. And hey, you can have some of my luck for the drawing, eh?" He pulled out a dollar bill that had been scribbled on with a red Sharpie. "I got a good feeling about tonight."

She wagged her finger as she walked away from him. "I'm holding you to that."

*

Diego walked out of Hidden Atlantis, turned southwest on Jackson Lane, and disappeared into the darkness of a black walking trail.

To him, it felt like a normal walk, only a couple hundred paces or so from the casino, and on a night five degrees below zero, even that short amount of time should've been numbing his skin.

But beneath the ice on the ground, layers of frozen soil led into layers of cold gravel and rocks, a kingdom of cold sand. He could feel them as he passed, his steps gliding long and quick across the land, as if his whole form was pulled by the wind.

The old man had told him there was no area in the land he hadn't explored or run his fingers over. He claimed to have been around since the dawn of time, but Diego had his doubts. For one, the flicker in his eyes whenever he stared at a screen, the pounds of lined skin hanging from his face in greeting back. He could see some amazement at the glow. The sandman's eyes grew in excitement at any piece of technology that Diego used, and something about that felt more juvenile than ancient.

For another, whenever he dreamed, those whispers crawling across his skin had the voices of recent history, ones whose regrets circled over and over in his mind to the melody of modern life. The moans of men and women in their sunset years, all their savings feeding into the machines, young men with dreams of glory and championship in the cards, and so many children whose minds were ripped apart and in solace looked to the bright lights of worlds that could be delivered by glass.

The sandman's oldest victims flickered inside the casino walls for only brief moments and in confusion left just as quick. The ones who stayed had reason to.

Beneath his feet, far north of a city called Kildere, the graves of Igra, Gregory, and Wovoka Moose.

Diego looked up above. "Does your mount still have some juice in him?"

A bolt of pale green lightning answered him, striking the ground but snaking away from his boots. He knelt and threw large clumps of warm muck over his shoulders.

The deeper he went, the more the cold grains ran through his fingers like never-melting snow, leaving dark stains on his hands, biting veins of pain under the skin and

I opened my eyes, dear brother. And my ears, mother, father, though I don't think what I learned should be any comfort as you rise.

Dear Igra, through whispers I've heard and felt the burn of your prosperous hopes. Your soul certainly had enough leftover credit.

It's a shame your spin on this medicine roulette came afoul of my sandman. He severed your floral stems long before I'd come around, mother, to be sure neither of your spirits could take root. Whether Great Spirit sent or whether Great Spirit tossed you ashore in this sea of reels, whether sacral seed or simple syrup, you two would always play the straw dolls.

And if there's always puppetry afoot where the jobs are posted, why shouldn't I get a tug?

On the machines, quit while you're ahead, but in an office on the rez, take all you can get.

How, you might ask, Wovoka, how does your last of kin, your last hope for remembrance, get so twined in all this netting? So caught in the dreamcatcher's sticky strands? So tethered to the sand of one shadowed old man?

You never heard what their whispers had to say about Igra, buried one.

Halfway into the grave, I can feel the shape of your resting box even now, the layered lines of this soil as it's been taking in the rainwater and freezing in this land's winter hell. Roots of grass through my knuckles tell me they grow to avoid what they know is below. But I've not the fear of grass in my veins, brother. There's much difference in us that way, fellow lost one.

When you flew away from us, you doomed her, Wovoka. You knew I wouldn't have the patience to stay, yet you left first and had the gall to scream my name in blame at her funeral. How self-important. How masturbatory in absolution.

Then you came back, and none of the whispers could ever matter to you, but just know this as my fingers touch the soft corners of your underground shelter: I hear everything. I know your secrets, and oh, oh, it brings a pain to my ears and a twinge in my neck that will kill me one day, but I know the ugliest depths of the land. Never forget it.

Oh, but we are not of these silly river people. No friend to water I've been, though very soon I may swim.

There are so many roads that don't exist anymore, brother. Not underneath this future parking lot, not under the black-and-yellow maze of Atlantis, no, but somewhere. And its own winding roads still exist, a great land where a people once sparked.

We were hunters once, in the shadow of the great bay where the miigis *shell rose. That's what they whisper to me, the ghosts of our family's past. They tell us our blood was on the land where the yellow birds sang. Where our people's great vision might've flourished, were it not for the vile unknown who festered.*

Is that what you are, Sandman? Did you come from there? Oh, don't get angry now. Even you whisper in your sleep when you're not weeping at a lake.

Igra, I bring you back in the spirit of love, in hopes you will find some heaven in Atlantis.

Wovoka, I want you to taste this one-dollar token and come back angry.

In these dark hours of a new year, will my family come back anew?

A spin at the reels requires coin, casino's obol, when there's nothing left to lose.

*

Diego placed the blood-stained casino token inside his brother's jaw. Through his eye sockets, a blue glow—the same one he could sense emanating from the grave one plot over—and something from beyond rushed back into his brother's body.

"Yes, Wovoka. Pay your way back to this life."

He paused and then sighed. Looking down from the grounds Diego had thoroughly unhallowed, the sandman laughed.

"As with the house, I always win, Diego."

The haunted house always wins.

"Now you see. But no longer with your own eyes, as you'd hoped. That was hope I tasted inside you, yes?"

Eh. It's like any other turn at the reels. I had a little hope. But, not really, ya know?

"Sing with me, child. The ghosts go dancing one by one, hurrah, hurrah."

The slot machines have won by one, hurrah, hurrah.

Beneath his feet, the casket shook. Blood spurted to the back of his throat as his teeth dug deep into his tongue. The ground underneath gave way, and both brothers were swept away in a cold, subterranean current.

Diego tried to scream, but the scraping and grinding of cold dirt filled his mouth. He felt several teeth get pulled straight out of his head as craggy boulders and bedrock rushed over his body.

For miles, the torrent of dirt dragged the bodies of the Moose family. When the shifting stopped, Diego felt his consciousness returned to a raw and pulsing body of pain. He could sense his brother nearby, and Igra, and dozens of others, swirling downward into the ground in a wide tornado of body and bones.

He could hear, far above this spiraling soil tomb, the clinking bells and whistles of the slot machines.

PART THREE

Noddingham

The sun in your eyes made some of the lies
worth believing.

—"Eye in the Sky,"
THE ALAN PARSONS PROJECT

Chapter 13   ☠   THE IMPROVED ORDER OF RED MEN

MARION LAFOURNIER

I walk into Indian Hollow from the south road, where the exit from the highway comes in. About a half mile from the city proper, there's a small motel called the Norway Pine Inn. From the outside it looks like a simple place without many amenities, but after I rent a room with some of my travel cash, I find it comes with a relatively modern TV and a tablet with a few video game apps, most of them a blur of vibrant colors and game options. There's even a credit card extension in case I want to put funds right into the game.

Instead, I use the forest-green ballpoint pen and small pad of peel-away notes next to the phone and try to recall my mother's phone number. The memory is foggy through the lingering migraine from waking up in a ditch in the winter, but I manage to write down the few numbers I do remember. Mom, Dad, and a weepy ex. No one stopped to check on me, but hey, that's the rez. They probably assumed I was just another homeless vagrant and averted their eyes. Even when I lived off rez in Half Lake that was the reflex of most townsfolk.

It's been a long time since it's felt important to remember a number. Smart phone spoiled, still. Of all the things I've seen in the past year, a house with a landline ranks high on the paranormal list.

I try my mother's number, but it's the voice of some office aide to one of those mall-side investment firms. My stepfather's number is also wrong, the automated voice claiming what I'd called is a number no longer in service, something I doubted Anni would let slip.

I wouldn't try Shannon's number even if I was confident I knew it, which is increasingly turning into doubt as I look at the motel's mint-green customized Post-its. I flip it over and read the logo on the back, the address and awkwardly placed social media tags of some office products company in a Minnesota city I've never even heard of. It could be down the road, could be in a bustling farm town, could be in the metro. Even if I had an idea to identify it by zip code, the numbers on this side are looking just as blurry as my scribblings on the other. They look as if they want to crawl away.

I stagger to the bathroom mirror. I've looked worse on a hard night of drinking a time or two, but for certain I'm not my best. Beet-red eyes, wide pupils, and three fading scratches across my cheeks. Like the faintest memory of a cat's wary swat, scabs days old, sunken into the skin in deep burgundy ink. When I rub at these scars, they slowly fade, so slow their initial presence almost feels like a trick of the long florescent tube above the mirror, the plastic cover nowhere in sight. When I glance up at the light and back, the pale walls glower in deep fuchsia-purple and green in the light's wake. I stumble back to the bed, settle in under the heavy blankets, and sleep again. This time the darkness is placid, soundless, and relaxing.

*

When I wake up, the alarm clock reads 10:00 a.m. My mouth is dry, and the headache lingers.

I crawl out of the motel bed and spend the next half hour in the bathroom, glad to have warm, salt-treated water. The refreshing combination of soap, toothpaste, and alcohol mouthwash push the headache away.

The motel is only a few blocks from the main street of Indian Hollow, a place of tall brick buildings, craggy and faded, as old as they look. Most have their original business name carved into the stone, banks and bars, textiles, groceries, appliances, and furniture, and below, their innards have been replaced with modern shops, boutiques, consignments, gift shops, bookstores, cafes, and between those, more modern versions of some of the original services. A town in and out of time, and confidently so.

I stop in a gas station in between the downtown area and another county highway, hoping they'll have a basic contract cell phone or even a flip phone for sale. I find a bottle of ibuprofen and a good sale on my brand of energy drinks but no phone services. And of course, a box of cigarettes, my brand, but almost three dollars more than at the casino gift shop. The back half of the gas station has a small selection of clothes, enough to comfortably replace the contents of my blasted car.

Outside, the blare of a train horn cuts across the sky, passing behind the gas station, holding up lines of traffic through the downtown exit.

I double back to the motel and change into the new clothes before further exploring this tranquil little town.

Between a candy store and a pipe tobacco shop, there's a gray brick building with a blue-and-white star quilt in the

window and black decals on the outside that read LODGE OF
THE IMPROVED ORDER OF RED MEN.

In smaller, almost fine-print decals in the corner of the
building, it read MEETINGS EVERY MONDAY NIGHT. FIND US
ONLINE! with a QR code taped to the glass.

Back in Half Lake and Geshig, I know there were several masonic brotherhoods that popped up in history. They
seemed to come in with or hot on the heels of the lumberjack
companies. Maybe they were one and the same. But it seemed
like they lived in a limbo area. I've never known anyone who
attended the church, but I've met people who've said they did,
and at the same time, that feels odd to think about because
that's pretty much how every church worked for me growing up. All the churches were strangers, yet at the same time,
all the people we knew were not strangers, and the churches
weren't strangers to them. In the exaggerated claims across
movie screens and conspiracy books, masonic brotherhoods
were the stuff of clandestine wonder, the triangular menace
on the dollar, the gatekeepers of all knowledge. They were
also just down the road.

I wander a few more aimless blocks until the train passes
by, and when it does, I see a small, squat building with old
and fire-burned wooden pillars, faded red bricks, and a neatly
tiled roof. An old railroad station converted into a museum.
There's one in every American town.

The second time I saw an animal die, it was near the train
tracks in Geshig. The buses were leaving school, and ahead
of ours, a bus driving parallel to the tracks ran over a straw-
brown pit bull mutt, and the kids on the bus got a harsh view
of a dog's stomach. The first time was also near those same
train tracks. I'd wandered off from my mother and her friends
during a neighborhood stroll and being probably no older

than four, I had no sense to avoid the rusty tracks. I wandered close to a dirt road crossing among some bushes, and nearby I saw a massive eagle with tarnished, crooked, and bent wings, a face full of anguish and desperate pleading. Whistly chirps for help. I didn't realize until way later that it was dying, not when it shuddered in front of me, at the same time my mother scooped me up and fled quickly from the sight.

I think of this when walking into the museum because straight ahead, next to the service counter, several taxidermized animals stare at me. A rampant brown bear, several eagles, and hawks in the wooden rafters above, and a few otters and muskrats sitting above a small model of a pond, shimmery black-green water made of some resin or epoxy.

"Ahoy!" the man behind the metal bars of the counter, the black twisted metal of fireplace instruments. "How are you today, bud?" A burnished gold name tag in a plastic placard near his elbow says his name is Dr. Ellison Baqaash.

"Doing okay. Visiting. Sightseeing."

"Where are you visiting from? Out of state?"

"Nah, just up the road, really. From this rez."

"Did you wanna tour the museum?"

"Uh, I guess not." I pause. "Actually, I was kind of curious about that lodge I saw on Walker Avenue. The Red Men?"

The man behind the counter sighs and shakes his head. "What a name, right? And on a reservation, no less."

"Seems like someone might've suggested changing it."

"Oh, a handful of times, but I've heard that when it's been broached, voices representing the Languille Lake tribe usually speak in favor of keeping it."

"What kind of voices?"

"Native veterans, mostly."

"Oh, I see." I pause and glance around the train station.

The name of the town is carved into the wood on the banister above the doorway. "Come to think of it, why is the town still called Indian Hollow? Swear I heard something about people wanting to change that back in high school."

"Maybe in the last year or two, but it's pretty much the same reason as the lodge."

"Makes sense. So is the lodge active, or is that, like, part of this museum?"

The man laughs and opens the hinged countertop to step out from behind the square desk. He walks straight to me. "We're active. You could read about it in our library if you'd like."

Ellison shakes my hand and leads me to a wide office in a side room, one with tall rectangular windows, making it brighter than the rest of the old train station, with its oil-pitch walls and vaulted ceiling. All the books are kept on three shelves shaped like half a canoe and one standard library cart next to them.

"Is that real birchbark?"

"It certainly could be," Ellison says with a wink. "If it's lodge chapters you're looking for, I'd start there. I'll leave you to it."

"Do you have any scratch paper?"

"Over on the desk."

"Thanks."

Ellison walks back to his post. On the shelf he gestures to a row of grainy books with those old scratchy, fiber-bound covers. One is some kind of coupon book and advertisement catalog. The first mention of these Red Men is from a page of local lodge listings from 1937, along with names like Knights of Columbus, Sons of Norway, American Legion, Orders of Eagles, Elks, and even Druids. I think the closest I've ever been to something like this was in a gay club in the cities, where one of the dungeons was full of pup players and other animal activities.

There's a handful of meeting minutes from the Indian Hollow Red Men bound in a cheap plastic spiral with a single laminate page on the front. I flip through it, but there's not much but a lot of hem-hawing, ideas put forth, and so many of those meeting motions, approvals, and yeas and nays, mostly involving potluck planning. Nothing all that interesting.

The shelves look to be arranged by topic. Minnesota towns, general Minnesota history, and Ojibwe history. One I recognize from high school years: *Chippewa Customs* by Frances Densmore. We read this chapter by chapter in an Indigenous studies class, but my fourteen-year-old mind didn't comprehend the style well. I pick it up and just a small glance inside is enough to see it was written in another era. Grainy letters on yellowed parchment, a weak spine barely holding it together.

In the middle, someone's left a construction paper bookmark. Page 98, in a section called Stories and Legends. The first subsection within is called "Story of the first earth."

A pair of glowering nickel-ball eyes pop up in my memory. Carey Ataage, my stepdad's medicine man friend. At some point in his smoke-filled, financed sauna he retrofitted into a sweat lodge, I could swear his eyes started to burn in colors brighter than his spirit fire. Sevenfire sight. That's what Alana called her gift.

The Ojibwe walk in four worlds.

Back in the summer of this year, Kayden's spirit showed me one of these worlds, one where he hadn't been viciously murdered by a Haltstorm boy and he's grown into the protector of the town he'd aspired to be.

The book in front of me casts the people of the first earth

as unwise and unlearned, only saved by the grace of the Creator's holy spirit Ockabe'wis, who taught them everything. It ends introducing Winabojo. In school we knew him as Wenaboozhoo the silly hero.

I was lucky enough to attend a school where Ojibwe was a required course throughout, and more than half a dozen teachers and assistants over the years all seemed to believe the same thing about where the cultural hero was.

A giant walleye ate him. That's where he lives.

It was a sturgeon the size of an ichthyosaur. Those were around when Wenaboozhoo was born.

He walked into a muskie's mouth one day and still lives there.

I yawn and run my left hand through my hair. "If I knew how to fish, I could just have him deal with this sandman."

A chair and floorboard creak in the nearby office.

"Hmm? What's that, bud?"

I look over and see Ellison craning his neck in the doorway, the leather office chair sticking back about forty-five degrees to the floor.

"Nothing." I drop my arm and bury my face back into the book. "Just mumbling to myself. Taking some notes."

"Whatcha reading about?"

"Eh. Just some legends. Creation myth stuff, the usual."

On the office wall behind him, there's a small poster of a man with some gadget in his hand like a pistol, camera in his other, surrounded by gray blobs with hints of faces. *Hunt for the Paranormal.* There's a logo of some television channel in the corner.

I motion with my lips to the wall. "You a ghost hunter?"

"Not myself, but helped out an adventurer or two. With different properties and historical questions about them."

"Did you guest star in that show?"

"Nah, I'm not pretty enough for that. Just an answers guy."
He winks. "Bet he'd have hired you."

I laugh through my nose and shake my head. "Nah, I don't interview well. Could say I'm on a paranormal quest of my own, though."

"Oh yeah? Lemme guess." He walks to the shelf, rubbing his temples and humming. "Mm, this one!" The book in his hand is a thin hardcover with a black-and-white photo of an old building on the front. "*Life Interrupted: Visions of Minnesota During the Tuberculosis Pandemic.* This one's popular with the ghost hunters. Has a lot of photos of the sanitorium up the road."

"Nah, that's boring."

"Hah! Boring? What's boring about it?"

"Any old-ass building can be haunted. Especially that one. Yeah, lots died there, sure, so there's not much mystery, right?"

"Only if you find old ghosts boring."

"Could be an old ghost. Hard to say. Have you ever been to the casino in Waubajeeg?"

"Oh, I think for a work lunch maybe, but I'm not really a gambler."

"Me neither. But some friends told me it's haunted. Piqued my interest a little."

"Heh. One of the paranormal hunters I worked with once said he'd love to bring a crew to a casino's hotel. Any one, didn't matter which, but he said all of them would decline on the spot. They're a little camera shy."

"Only other people's cameras." I stand next to him in front of the shelf. "My friends think something is after the casino, but they don't think it's a ghost."

"What do they think it is?"

"Something worse. It's a presence old and ancient. They're not sure if it's a danger."

"Hmm."

Ellison puts back the photograph book and pulls out a wide paperback titled *A History of the Ojibway People* by a writer named William W. Warren.

"If it's old and ancient you want, I think I know where you should start."

He flips through and finds a passage that someone has already highlighted and marked up. I sit back down at the table and read. Ellison opened the book to chapter 6, titled "Dispersion of the Ojibways from the Island of LaPointe."

The first section details the Ojibwe pushing the Dakota west toward the Mississippi and then moves into a grisly account that older men of the author's era were not fond of talking about.

According to other accounts, the dispersion of the Ojibways from the island of their refuge, was sudden and entire. The Evil Spirit had found a strong foothold amongst them, during the latter years of their residence on this island. Evil practices became in vogue:—Horrid feasts on human flesh became a custom. It is said by my informants, that the medicine men of this period had come to a knowledge of the most subtle poisons, and they revenged the least affront with certain death. When the dead body of a victim had been interred, the murderer proceeded at night to the grave, disinterred it, and taking it to his lodge he made a feast of it, to the relatives, which was eaten during the darkness of midnight, and if any of the invited guests became aware of the nature of the fest, and refused to eat, he was sure to fall under the ill-will of the feaster, and become the next victim. It is said that if a young woman refused the addresses of one of these medicine men, she fell a victim to his poison, and her body being disinterred, her relatives were feasted on it by the horrid murderer.

Such a taste did they at last acquire for human flesh, that parents dared not refuse their children if demanded by the fearful medicine men for sacrifice. And numerous anecdotes are related of circumstances happening during this horrid period, which all tend to illustrate the above assurances, but which the writer has not deemed proper to introduce, on account of the bloody and unnatural scenes which they depict. The Ojibways, at this period, fell entirely under the power of their Satanic medicine men, and priesthood, who even for some time caused themselves to be believed to be invulnerable to death. This, however, was finally tested one night, by a parent whose beloved and only child had just fallen victim to the insatiable longing for human flesh, of one of those poisoners. After interring his child, he returned at night with his bow and arrow and watched near the grave. At midnight he saw what appeared to be the form of a black bear, approach and commence digging into the grave. It was also believed that these medicine men possessed the power of transforming themselves into the shapes of animals.

But the determined father, overcoming his fear, launched his barbed arrow into the body of the bear, and without waiting to see the consequence of his shot, he fled to his wigwam. The next morning, the body of one of the most malignant and fearful poisoners was found clothed in a bearskin, weltering in his blood, on the grave of the old man's child, whom he had made a victim.

The author takes a paragraph to speculate on whether this nightmarish era was the direct result of a crop famine, and the trace of the old skeptic inside me wants to side with this explanation, but my shaking hands tell me that impulse has no power here.

It is further stated that these evil practices were carried on to such an extent, that the Che-bi-ug, or "souls of the victims," were at last heard nightly traversing the village, weeping and wailing. On this the inhabitants became panic stricken, and the consequences was that a general and complete desertion of the island of their refuge took place, which left their town and fields entirely desolate, and from that time, they have become overgrown with trees and bushes, till scarcely a vestige of their former site is to be seen.

How far the nightly weeping of the dead, which caused this sudden fear and panic, was drawn from the imagination of the wicked inhabitants, or originated in the nightly secret wailings of fond parents for victimized children, we are not able to affirm, certain it is however, that from that time, the Ojibways considered the island as haunted, and never resided on it till after the first old French traders had located and built their trading establishment thereon.

I look up at Ellison.

"Who underlined this?"

"I don't know for sure, but the only person I remember with the book before I found it like this is one of the men you're searching for. Since then, he's become the grand chair of the Red Men." He smiles. "I could introduce, if you'd like, but you'd have to wait until Monday night."

Old face, nightmare face. Maybe now he's moved on to a puppet with a handsome face.

"I've got a little time in town to spare. I can come."

*

I spend the next few days sitting in my motel room, flipping through the TV. Several times now I've tried to remember phone numbers and passwords I might use to get ahold of family. Every time I try, there's at least one character that's different written down from what I recall in my head, but whenever I notice, I can't remember what I originally thought it was. Eventually, the migraine comes through with ugly green flashes when I close my eyes and rub down hard on my temples and forehead.

I check my face for those purple marks the sandman left, but there's nothing. I inspect myself all over for any other signs, but as far as I can see, it's gone. Same me, same general shape. Few nights of good rest have me looking less ragged, and there's a triple-lined scar on my right cheek, but nothing like that first day.

I've spent about a hundred of the jackpot dollars in my wallet on medication at a local drugstore, but every OTC solution has only mitigated for a couple hours or so. It's an awful brain fog I can't shake, and when it's at its peak, the lines in the wood-paneled walls of the motel room look as if they're shaking and shivering with each pulse of blood through my temples and neck.

By Monday morning, the migraine's gone away, but what's replaced it is a sort-of shaking emptiness. Not of mood, but somewhere halfway between my skin and I guess my thoughts and my heartbeat, there's something that I can't feel, and what accompanies it is like a fever shake, but my body isn't sweating. Just to be cautious, I buy a cheap ear thermometer at the drugstore on my third trip, but each time I check it is right where it should be.

The last thing I think to do is take a long jog out in the mid-November cold. It'd been a snowy weekend, but nothing too icy. I jog on the south side of town, where a long walking trail surrounds a park and a canal that leads to a bay on Lake Truthwaite. I run a few miles until the feeling of being out of breath in the stale air outweighs that unknown untethered feeling.

Back at the motel, another long, hot shower helps my skin breathe, and slowly the emptiness fades.

An hour after I dry off, there's a knock at my door.

"Mr. Lafournier?"

"Hey." I zip up the gas-station sweater and open the door.

"Ready to meet some Red Men?"

"Why not."

On the way he tells me about the circumstances that brought him from the northwest coast to a reservation in Minnesota. He'd been a student of history and pedagogy but only finished half a graduate degree before settling in Indian Hollow as the art director for the museum. He was going to go back eventually but fell in love with the area and out of love with academic deadlines and paper grading.

Two streets away from the Red Men's lodge, I see a bar called Babs' Big Bar & Bingo. I stop and stare, my confusion at the sight reupping traces of the migraine.

"How can there be bingo here?" I ask.

"Indian Hollow and Languille Lake have a partnership for profits at this particular bingo hall."

"I thought Waubajeeg and this town hated each other."

"For high school sports and tourist bucks, sure, but in the end, money grooms pragmatism. And that can outweigh any arbitrary tribal line."

Outside the Lodge, Ellison holds the door open and bids me in with a playful bow. Inside there are three rows of long folding tables covered in white plastic. A dozen and a half men sit about the lodge and all look in my direction as I walk in.

"Welcome, brothers," says a man sitting on top of the table near the back. "We're just about to start. Who's your new guy, Mr. Baqaash?"

"This is Marion. Ghost-hunting straggler I found in the library at the station."

"Welcome," the man says. He's a tall Indian with long gray-and-black hair, a maroon pullover sweater, eyes like he just smoked a joint, and a jaw bigger than my own head. "I'm Makwade, grand chair of these Red Men. All seekers of knowledge are welcome here, so long as they believe in a force far greater than their own."

"I was just telling Marion that you both gravitated to the same book." Ellison looks at me and winks, another friendly smile spreading across his scruffy face.

I slowly turn from the museum curator to the grand chair. "I wouldn't say I *believe* in a greater force. I've seen a couple, though."

Makwade chuckles, and the men around me join in, nudging each other with elbows and yeah-yeahs.

"We at the lodge only require one thing: the ultimate sharing of wisdoms. All of us have belief and a submission to that belief, whether this looks like a Christian god or any other, including the universe and science. What power have you witnessed that you might share with us, Marion?"

All eyes turn to me. I hesitate before blurting out, "I'm mostly just looking for leads on a spirit."

Makwade lifts his hands out and above his shoulders. "Well, there it is. Tell us of your spirits, brother."

"Well. Actually, I don't know if it's a *spirit* spirit. Last summer, I was pretty sure I saw a spirit for the first time. It came to me in the body of a dog. Or wolf. One of those hybrids you hear about on the rez all the time. But it went away once I helped it, and I figured I wouldn't see it again. But just yesterday I thought I saw the spirit of . . ." I look all around, and the eyes are still focused on me, Ellison's smile growing ever wider. "A relative. A great-uncle. But I was wrong. It wasn't him. It was something pretending to be him."

Makwade leaned forward, a wide paw of a hand resting on his devil's tower chin. "What do you mean *pretending*?"

"Like he was wearing my grandfather's image, like a Halloween costume. But it wasn't just him. There were these ugly imitations of ghosts all throughout the car. Just. Just losing it, crying and freaking out. And when he was talking about them, he called them *manidookaazo*. Said they were just pretending to be spirits."

"But what has the power to pretend to be a spirit and be so convincing?"

I shrug. "Who knows."

"Exactly. It's a mystery." Makwade stands up, hands on his hips. "Mysteries surround us, and they flow in all directions. Good, bad, and every infinite direction between and outside of that plain. When I was a child, my mentor told me there are four worlds the Ojibwe will walk through, and each one we should try to meet with dignity and courage."

My eyes go out of focus as he speaks, but Ellison discreetly nudges my bicep with his own. I try to focus on his waxing, but on the wall behind him I can see a series of Native American–themed motivation posters, ones I might've seen back in high school. Seven Indian Commandments, Red Footprints, the like. But one is a stoic yet proud-looking man in buckskin and braids, paddling a canoe through stalks of wild rice. At the top is the word *manoomin* in bold yellow, with a smaller translation beneath it: The Good Grain.

Ellison whispers in my ear, "You know, we can make this as interesting as you want it to be." He drags his fingertips across my chest and up to my chin softly. "Men with a vice play Minnesota nice."

In a tense unison, the men of the lodge reach for their shirts and buckles. Flannel unbuttons top to bottom. Fishermen's hats are cast away, along with wool gloves, steel-toed boots, and dingy leather work gloves. Most of the men's faces freeze, a glaze of trembling dissociation awash in their eyes as they're forced to disrobe by some unseen and sick force.

Ellison titters. "What? You don't think it'll be good, with all these lumberjacks? Who better to handle this . . . ?"

I grab his wrist and push it away before he can travel downward.

Sweat drips down my neck, and my pulse quickens as more of my body heats up. I can feel my fingers and toes tremble like I drank too much coffee with not enough food. Thinking about food, I scan the room and see there's a big platter of cheese and crackers, a pot of some grayish soup, and simple turkey sandwiches on white bread cut in half diagonally.

I run over to the table and grab a sandwich, nibble at it quickly, and reach for a generic bottled water to wash it down. I feel Ellison join me at the table, a soft chuckle as he claps me on the back.

"I was getting worried."

"How long?" I say in heavy breaths between bites. "How long is too long?"

"Don't worry. You're fine. You saw past his weavings, and you finally remembered to eat."

I look back into the crowd, and most of the men look more confused than aware of what Ellison had said. A few didn't flinch. Some are still in the early stages of undress, embarrassment apparent in their ears, but they slowly readjust their clothes and turn their focus back to their own business.

At the back corner of the room, four slot machines fade into view. The men who sit in front of their blue screens had started to undress with all the others, but that look in their eyes is not for the circumstance. Their minds are only for the reels.

"Is this Atlantis?"

"No," Ellison replies. "The number of games in this lodge is fractional compared to those hallowed halls in Waubajeeg. As are my little glamours to his threads."

The food drops into my stomach like a sack of bricks, but with each bite my heart rate drops and my frenzied mind is gentled. But all at once the sandman's ugly visions flood through my mind's eye, and I turn to the group of staring men. Most are confused, but some look empathetic and solemn.

"Do any of you collect state quarters?" I ask.

One by one the men fumble for their wallets, and eyes are wide and unblinking when over a dozen red-painted quarters come out. I back away from the tables and make for the door.

"What's going to happen when I leave?" I cautiously shout back at the man sipping the bowl of hominy soup.

"We'll be here. We've still got a few agenda items to take care of. Upcoming Christmas party. Either gonna rent the bowling alley in Kildere or the movie theater in Half Lake.

Hasn't been put up for a vote just yet." Ellison approaches me just as I reach the threshold of the temple door and speaks softly. "The men here are quite real, Marion. Some just fall into his design easier than others." He brings his hands in front of his face and twiddles his thumbs. "I've never been able to get the hang of beadwork. But the sandman knows beadwork older than any book you'll find in my library."

I run out of the door and don't stop until I reach the gas station. I buy a pint of milk and a greasy burger wrapped in foil with a layer of what feels like the thinnest possible width for bacon.

It tides me over while I get back to the motel. In the bathroom mirror, I see the three purple thorns that had attached to my skin have returned. I peel them off and drop them in the water of the motel toilet. A pinprick pain inside my ear starts to ring. From the canal comes a fourth thorn in between my thumb and index fingertip.

There's still a migraine, but the shaking emptiness recedes as I flush them all.

Chapter 14   ☠   NODDINGHAM

LIAM HALESTORM

February 5, 2018

Liam Haltstorm's first drink was cheerleader beer in a cheerleader's basement, and to combat his supreme disappointment in the quality, both taste and of mind, he vowed to drink only better-quality poison each time after.

He used to keep a tally of each time he broke the vow on the back of a punch card, but one night after a box of purple-pink bliss, he cleaned out his wallet and noticed the card had no marks on it. Only a few more punches before a free latte, though.

Seven years later, a grim twenty-six upon him, Liam sat at the greasy bar top in Hidden Atlantis, nursing a Long Island iced tea, wondering what kind of latte he might get next on that fruitless coupon quest. Wondering why the worst drink he'd had on his twenty-first birthday tasted like the best only half a decade later.

What liquor doesn't taste like Torani after Suboxone strips?

The how seemed pretty simple to him. When the drink didn't work, the weed worked, and when the weed didn't work, the molly worked, and when the work fell behind, the gabapentin worked, and when the gabapentin worked, more gabapentin really worked, and when still more gabapentin no longer worked, everything together worked, and then when every other thing worked, the oxycodone worked even better after he broke his leg, the result of a clumsy fall off his uncle's porch, and when the oxycodone stopped flowing, the worst thing worked, and then the worst thing that stops the true worst thing rescued him before his heart stopped doing its work.

What bugged him most was how fast it all went when so much of it was just the comfort of a moment, just a few minutes where he could slow down and think.

"Refill?" the bartender asked.

"No, thank you," Liam said.

He went back to the room on the first floor near the end of the hall, where he'd been living the past month. His mother had demanded he move out because his promise of sobriety was a slow one.

Slow and steady, and it hurt him more than getting kicked out by his own parent that he couldn't talk to Alana.

The casino floor felt so different, so quiet without her or Cherie. Even jerkass Zach's absence made the atmosphere worse.

Now, whenever he sat at the slots, any bank, any day, his compatriots were as quiet and reserved as he—and they all seemed to have the same trouble staying awake as he did. But at least Alana's blond sasquatch wasn't there to annoy him and scrutinize his every mood.

Something about that white guy always sat wrong with Liam, and even though plenty of the Native guards enforced the rules about as strict as Zach, it still felt less abrasive when they told him to stop nodding off.

Liam rifled through the piles of mail on the hotel room's table and found the promotional coupons he'd received in the mail, five of them totaling fifty dollars to spend over the next week.

It was his last before he walked out of the casino forever. Well, forever as a guest. And still, only this site, once he got his job. Even this far north, there were casinos in all directions.

He exchanged all five coupons at once, which came with a five-dollar penalty, but still, forty-five more dollars he didn't have.

Near the poker tables, Liam settled in an empty bank of machines called *Lucky Lotus Land* and watched as rows of pink and white flowers passed by on golden tile reels.

The finality of this round of gambling became apparent to him when he was still playing off of the forty-five promo dollars from earlier, sometimes winning enough to want to cash out, sometimes getting anger-inducingly low before bouncing back up. It wanted him to teeter right around forty, but a win would come. He knew it.

He lit a cigarette and, noticing how dry his mouth had become, scanned around the area for any service carts. Didn't look like anyone was on duty, so he tilted his chair forward against the lotus screen and fetched a big cup of cola before sitting down and losing it all again.

*

Two migraine-filled, sober days later, Liam suffered through the first full day of what was to be a two-week orientation process. At a desk with a complimentary notepad with the casino logo on the front and a pencil made from cedar that read MAGIC MIDNIGHT CASINO & SUITES, Liam stared into the blue lines on white and couldn't imagine a worse hell than trying to detox while feeling as if he were back in school.

According to the clock, they were two and a half hours in when Liam finally zoned back in to the orientation leader's words.

"The next form is our provider's double indemnity contract. You can name one or multiple next of kin."

The thought caused Liam to clench his fists tight, and he used the tip of his thumb to push the pencil's eraser over the metal casing until it stretched and detached from the top. The same provider denied the Haltstorm family's claim on Cherie, citing her death as an accidental overdose. No one knew why she'd followed her brother and father to the same cold road after so many years of clear skies.

A few of the more hot-headed Haltstorms made this their final straw with the company. *Never going to spend my money in this place again. Gonna go to the casino on the other rez or the other one on the other rez.* But Liam knew it wasn't their tribe's fault. The exact same thing had happened to his father when he was a teenager, and even though losing Cherie wasn't easy, he felt that and many other family tragedies had in some way braced, even groomed him to accept what he couldn't change.

*

A week into the job, Liam froze when he rounded the corner of a slot bank and saw Zach sitting in front of a keno machine. At present, patron, and on some other shift, current coworker, but no longer family. Alana leaned on him for the week of Cherie's funeral but left him and her job right after.

Zach stared at him with those popping blue eyes, and

Liam could see the stress of the past few months evident. The uncombed mess of yellow hair, uneven scruff building on his face. He wore loose jeans and a pale shirt, both covered in oily handprints.

After a few seconds of both clearly not wanting to be the first to speak, Liam took a quick breath and felt himself subconsciously stand up straighter. "Hey, man. Can I get you anything?"

Zach hesitated. Liam saw an untouched skewer of the tropical fruit at the bottom of the machine near his feet next to a half-empty coffee. He cleared his throat softly and then shook his head. "No, I'm good. Thanks."

Liam didn't hear any bitterness in his voice, but there was a gravelly quality to it that rankled his neck. Zach trying to speak soft sounded like a snoring pit bull. Liam nodded solemnly and continued down the aisle.

"Liam, wait."

He turned back. "Yeah?"

Zach scoffed and shook his head. "If they ask you to fetch the poker wrench, don't believe them. It's not real."

"Heh. Thanks for the heads-up," Liam said with a laugh. He turned away before his ears could betray him and make Zach realize it was too late to warn the now very sober but very gullible new guard.

*

For the next five hours, Liam's shift was spent answering phone calls at the back of the house. A slog of transfers and checking for lost-and-found items forgetful old folks and young stoners thought they'd left on the floor. Occasionally, a cell phone would receive a call in the secure cage where the lost items were left, the vibration rattling the rusted metal frame, Liam powerless to answer the call.

At the seven-hour mark, just an hour shy of leaving, an oncoming guard called in.

"We'll pay you OT if you can stay."

"Do I have to?"

Liam's main supervisor, a middle-aged Native guy with a permanently dejected face and bored tone, sighed and shook his head. "No, but I'd really appreciate it if you did. We need someone to make a supply delivery to Magic Midnight. If you don't stay till next shift, they won't have anyone with a license to bring it."

"None? Not one guard?"

"Yep."

"Why would they staff us like this?"

"I don't know, kid. That's just how the reservation clock works."

"Okay, I can stay."

Only a week sober did not feel like a state he should be trusted to transport supplies, especially since the majority of them were medical supplies for the casino EMT staff, but his license was clean despite himself, so he did as he was instructed.

It was an hour drive east to Magic Midnight in Kildere, the top-most side of the so-called Languille Lake Triangle. But even in one of the reservation's infamous bingo vans, nothing supernatural happened to him on the way there or back. No whispering stragglers, nothing his cousin Alana had described to him before.

Was sobriety really this clarifying? He'd never doubted Alana before, but the world around him was decidedly less mysterious and spiritual without the pills. *I guess Indian ghosts don't like boring men.*

When he dropped off the van and walked back into Hidden Atlantis, his supervisor said he would be fine to leave halfway through his second shift. He thanked him, clocked out, and made for the gift shop for a pack of smokes.

Tobacco in hand, he walked out of the cobalt-blue glass walls. Ahead of him, on the same keno machine, he saw Zach, still staring at the matrix of numbers and dots, deep red shadows under his gaping eyes. His cousin's once-fiancé had been on the machines for twelve hours. Undisturbed from his gaze to the screen, Zach didn't notice Liam quietly walk past and pick up a series of small, crumpled wads of paper around his chair.

ATM withdrawal slips, in increasing amounts by the time stamps. Forty dollars, then fifty, then a hundred dollars, two, three. Adding up to thousands spent since the morning shift. Liam tossed the slips in the trash and walked off the casino floor without a word.

*

Two months on the job, he got a 1.2 percent raise. It was only fifteen cents, but it was the first time he'd ever stayed at a job long enough to earn one.

Life was clearer for him internally, but Atlantis was as shrouded in smoke as ever. In the time since taking the job, he'd added blueberry cough drops to his daily hard candy stores. Spring was near, and with a heavier customer load, more smoke would be able to linger thicker than the air system could deal with. On top of the usual humidity that came with northern summers, he thought for the first time in his life maybe he was missing Minnesota winters.

It was in the late hours of the morning when Liam rounded the corner between the back two walls of the casino and overheard two of his fellow guards chatting about a suspected drug dealer.

"I saw him over at Noddingham again."

"Might know. Prime real estate for his type, eh?"

"What's that?" Liam said as he approached.

Both of the guards seemed embarrassed and caught off guard. One was a tall Native guy, Boris Beaumacher, whom Liam vaguely remembered attending some school with. The other was a spritely nineteen-year-old girl named Vanina Dareville, whose lighter complexion could often give her embarrassment away, as it did currently. Boris was quick to jump into his phone and leave Vanina to respond to him.

"Oh, just something one of the floor guys started saying about the keno section."

Liam turned his head instinctively in the direction of the number games, and, recalling his own days of gambling there, he felt himself turn pale and then perhaps redden like she had. "Which guys?"

"Well, I don't really know who started it. Everyone was just saying it so casually lately." She shrugged, and her eyes darted around as if she were checking the floor for loose change.

"Yeah," Liam said, lightly clearing his throat. "Guess that's just the guys being guys."

He continued on, and his steps took him right to the keno section. The coworker who had trained him earlier in the year had advised him on the balancing of empathy and understanding with the need to have a fancy, professional business.

"Some days, the patrons will be happy," the trainer had said. "Can bet you'll see plenty of smiling faces. Might even catch them on a lucky day and get a little tip if they win. Other days, the gamers can look a lot different. Guess others have their philosophies, but I always tell people to be as patient as reasonably possible with our more troublesome guests."

At the keno section, beneath the chiseled stomach and sculpted arms of Poseidon, the screens were alight with bets and blue numbers. A handful of older ladies, the kind with big handbags and jewelry, were sitting in the crowd, nursing coffee and cigarettes while the red circles dotted the pixels. Not just older folk but patrons of all ages were not quite glued to the screens, for many were leaning back in their chairs, and some were half asleep. A girl who looked no older than twenty-five had one arm on the machine's edge, a shaky hand re-betting the card with her left arm crossed over, skeletal fingers tapping quicky against her right forearm. There were a few other tweakers in the crowd, shoulders, fingers erratic as their owners' eyes glowed blue and unblinking at their games of chance.

The sight reminded him he'd forgotten to take his gabapentin today. Liam woke the sleeping young woman with a light tap on her chair and asked if there was anything she needed. Soda, coffee, water? She shook her head and pulled up a big purple water bottle. "No, thank you, sir."

"Have fun, miss."

Liam let his supervisor know he was going for a smoke break. Before he left the floor, he stopped at the gift shop and picked up a pack of American Spirits. Out on the black tar of the back parking lot, he finished three before heading back to his locker for his forgotten dose.

It's still sobriety if my name is on the bottle.

Chapter 15 ☠ FOUR-DAY ROADS

MARION LAFOURNIER

Ellison knocks on my door around noon the next day but I don't answer.

"Marion. I need you to listen."

I'm sitting at the table, staring at the notes I remembered from the annals at the train station and the men's lodge. The vile unknown taking root on an island. An island demon's work, or holy work, and the setting sun on what was once a settlement with hope. The old men thought of it as auld lang syne, Makwade said. And they were familiar with the phrase only decades after the spark burned out. I write *weeping and wailing* at bottom of the notepad, between the final line and the paper company copyright information in fine print. Right above, *Che-bi-ug*. Souls of the victims.

Weeping and wailing. That's what the ghosts were doing when they were in my car. What they were trying to tell me. A haunting cry so piercing that it lived on in the nightmares of our people.

And all on the leash of this false and shifting sandman.

"We didn't know about him. Not at first, not consciously. Some of us still don't. Most are just there for a lodge experience. A brotherhood and bonding. I try to explain, now and then. But they zone out, and they don't hear me in the way I need them to. It's like we're all trying to write a letter at once, and even though we all know we're fully capable of language and communication, we all disagree on what exactly each letter of each word means. And even when we get to the bottom of that, well, let me tell you, there are some strong opinions out there on whether or not we should use cursive. Don't even get us started on whether all our emails should be in monospaced font. The conversation will end up where it always does. Lutefisk.

"Anyway. You need not worry. Indian Hollow is a genuine small-town American dream. There's everything you want, even though there's not much of anything. Like I said, you can still travel if you want. You can acclimate how you want. Unless you made him angry. Then I guess you'll have to ask for forgiveness or just wait until he's not mad. But what's time to a *manidoo*, eh?"

His footsteps on the crunchy snow fade away. I go to the door and open it. He's taped a folded printer paper onto the wood.

I open it and see a series of seven lines in an overlapping zigzag. It's a photocopy of an old facsimile that contains a drawing of the Ojibwe's Path of Life. A circle on the final line, just beyond the later intersection, is followed by Ellison's small, jagged writing on the bottom in blue ballpoint pen.

You're here. That's not so bad in a town with an art museum.

I crumple it up and throw it at the blue mesh wastebasket next to the TV stand/dresser.

The image of those four curved thorns swirling down the toilet keeps playing in my head.

The sandman is allegedly unable to come into Indian

Hollow, and if that weren't true, I don't know why I'd still be free, but if it is true, then a gaggle of mostly unsuspecting puppets would be a good workaround. And if the sandman has that much reach, that much power over the control and the chemicals in someone's body, a casino full of people on a reservation would look like a playground.

Da-da-da-da-da daaa daa.

I crawl back on the bed and wrap the body pillow around the top of my head. I apply soft pressure to my forehead and temple, and when I pull it away, only the vague tracings of a headache linger. I use the bed's remote to incline my back and then turn the built-in massage feature on low.

My car might be in bits on the road and my phone probably under the snow with it, but at least I had my wallet and jackpot winnings to buy me a comfortable place to rest.

I open my eyes, the popcorn ceiling above much less erratic than in the past few days.

I'm not much of a gambler. Too anxious. Still, it was some pretty good beginner's luck that I was able to win on my first trip inside in over six years.

Back at the bathroom mirror, my skin is looking less pale, and my eyes have cleared up. My irises are a bit too dark to truly judge if my pupils are back to normal, but what I can see of the outline suggests they're smaller.

"If I can get out of this, I'll never gamble again," I mutter as I put my arms behind my head and stretch them back. But first, one more gambit.

Out in the lobby, I check out of the motel and start walking, keeping the brochure of the area in my new jacket pocket.

The south side of town contains a lake that juts out just beyond Languille Lake's southern border. By now the lakes could be walkable. Could even be swimmable, or I could steal a boat. The map on the town brochure in the motel suggests it's not that big of a lake. If I could make it outside the reservation boundaries, could the sandman still follow?

Alana seemed to think his presence was limited between Waubajeeg and here, but if I'm wrong, if she's *been* wrong, then there's not much chance of escaping him anyway. He'll always be riding on that pitiful eagle's head, waiting for me to accept the inevitable and descend.

But for one last gambit, maybe not.

I bundle up in the gas station clothes and try to sink into them as much as possible, hoping it's making me look less conspicuous and not more. At least they can't see my face under the scarf. I head back to the south walking trail where I had jogged a few days ago and make my way toward Kirby Lake.

Less than a quarter mile onto the trail, I sense footsteps and spot a pursuer behind me.

It's Makwade from the men's lodge. By his much taller, lankier frame, I assume I wouldn't be able to outrun him. I turn back, a big gale of wind turning the trail and the white-and-green patterns of pine boughs and branches into a frenzy. Makwade's frame keeps still as he strode in a manner even the bigger trees couldn't manage.

"If you'd stayed for the full meeting, you'd know we're not a threat," he says on approach. He stops a few yards away. "We only want to help."

I throw my hands up and shake my head. "I have to admit defeat. I don't know what's real right now, and I have no way of knowing if I should trust your word. I'm at a point of pure gut instinct, and I wouldn't consider that a strong suit of mine."

"And I know that feeling. Mr. Baqaash has tried to explain

it all to me a few times. I was the same as you. Had an urge to visit the train station for some town history. And wouldn't you know it, the town was so interesting I never left."

"How did you realize it?"

"It was about a year in. One day it just occurred to me that I'd rearranged my whole damn life to continue my studies here. And it's not going so bad, either. Found a lot of our language between the train station, the library, and the city hall archives. The words of our people, captured either by inquisitive white settlers or by their own hands. But even though I realized something was wrong, and I can recall Mr. Baqaash's face moving as he tried to explain, all that my mind can comprehend is that it's a mystery."

I nod. "*Manidoo* means mystery. Does that help?"

"Child, do I look like a man who couldn't handle a spirit?" He laughs. "I suppose that's prideful of me. But were that the case, I wouldn't back down from a fight. If there was a *maji-manidoo* around, I would walk toward it with my arms wide open, ready to battle. But what's to battle? Ellison says there is one, but I don't feel it."

"I think I understand."

"I couldn't sleep last night when you left. What you called the *manidookaazo*." He shakes his head. "Cold as the lakes. What has the power to pretend to be a spirit? Nothing on my Creator's earth. Nothing made of the rocks and roots of Turtle Island."

"If I can find a way to leave this town, I can find a way to stop h—" I stop my breath from forming the word *him*. "I can find a way to handle the *manidookaazo*."

"I know of only one. It's not the way you're going."

"Any guidance is appreciated if you're sincere."

He turns his head to the right. "Like I said at the lodge,

dignity and courage. You'll need both if you're traveling west. I trust you know what I mean."

I shrug. "Danger in all direction, eh?"

"On the southwest side of Lake 35, there's a little grotto with a pile of boulders. When you get there, you'll see a door painted into the biggest one, in blue."

"What kind of door?"

"The kind of door that's old and ancient. Or not. It could be spray paint from the hardware store. But the last time I was there, it felt like it was calling to me."

"Like a door at the end of a hallway?"

"Like a mystery."

I pull out the brochure with the map and see the long, slender shape of Lake 35, like a paper clip bent into one bumpy line of wire. "Does it go outside the reservation boundary?"

"Good luck," he says with a nod. "Remember. Dignity and courage."

The tall *niij* strides past me, and though he doesn't come near enough to touch me, I still feel myself flinch a little. I hurry forward without looking back and head back into town to get to Lake 35.

*

The west end of town eventually thins into houses with open yards, the idyllic kind with a few bales of hay and porch swings, all covered with a coat of fluffy snow.

I follow County Road 200 southwest, and I feel the winter slowly reaching into my gas station clothes. If I hadn't bought them, there's a good chance I could've veered into hypothermia by now. Can't check a phone for temp instantly, but a sign with those red dot lights on a liquor store in town says it's around twelve degrees.

I've done better in worse weather before, but the past few days I was able to crank the heat in the motel, so my northern skin isn't quite up to par.

At the shore of the lake, I hesitate. It's covered in snow. I have no idea if the water's frozen yet. I let out a few bitter laughs because this is the exact sort of thing my ex Shannon would know about. He'd be calling me a bonehead about now if he saw me take these first steps.

My feet glide through the velvet snow like spreadable cheese, but they connect with what seems like a solid layer. Dignity and courage, he'd said. Never cared much about dignity before. In the closeted-to-coming-out process, youth to adult, there's really not much room for it. Most winters going out onto the ice would never be a consideration, even if a handsome man offered, but I make it halfway across without the urge to turn back.

The shivering could be nerves, but I choose to believe it's just the encroaching cold.

A biting wind with sideways snow hits from all sides out in the open lake, so I close my eyes, cover my face, and let my feet lead me where they will. Just like the only dream I've ever remembered. A door at the end of the hallway. A door that couldn't possibly open.

Through the violent slashes of wind, another grating sound cuts through. The piping whistle of a bald eagle's call.

By now my boots have soaked through, and my toes are numb, but I charge ahead across the lake as fast as my body will allow, leaving long, deep tracks in my wake.

I wouldn't be able to see him or his fetid steed through the snow, but I know he's there. I must've crossed out of the city's barrier or boundary. Whatever had been keeping him at bay, it has passed now, and I have one chance of escape.

In the thick line of gray, barren trees on the opposite shore, there's a slight dip on top, and sure enough, when I come crashing up near shore there's a trail through the woods. At the end of the grotto is a mound of gray granite boulders.

The snow's piled on thick, but in gaps where it hasn't quite taken over yet, I can see vibrant blue splotches.

I collapse in front of the boulder, my knees sinking into crunchy, frosty muck, and wipe away the snow to see a door smaller than my car windows. It doesn't budge as I pound against it with the side of my fists, and I feel silly for expecting anything different. I remove my gloves, stuff them in my jacket pocket, and pat the surface with my bare hands.

"Uh. Shit. *Biindigen!*" I blurt out. That's what our teachers in school would say when we walked into class. "*Biindigen! BIINDIGEN!*" I don't even know what it translates to.

I turn back and see the sandman descending, sending the eagle head back into the air with a violent stomp of its already blood-drenched eye hole.

The moment he lunges at me, talons of wrinkly skin inches from my neck, a small pair of hands grips my shoulders, and I fall backward, the snow-blind sky now just a speck of white as all becomes black once again.

Chapter 16 ☠ THE VILE UNKNOWN

GLENN NIELAN

February 22, 2018

G lenn didn't need to sell his camera equipment—he had more than enough savings to feed the beast—but he had an urgent need to get it out of the cabin. After the first ninety-six hours of uninterrupted, self-induced insomnia, he made up his mind. He took a half-day-long sleep and then brought them to an electronics store all the way in Half Lake. Then he went back to Hidden Atlantis for the usual.

In the first few spins of the golden reels, it felt right. Why had he cared so much about filming such a boring land anyway? As if it held anything more interesting than he could make it look like with a few clicks and some basic acoustic guitar and Indian flute samples. *Maybe even from the same pack as their hotel lobby music.*

It was only after another ten-hour session on a keno machine, when the last credits had trickled away and above him a thousand round black eyes reflected back at him in plastic mockery, that he regretted the sale.

Why? Why would you do that? he thought. *Why did you flush away your whole dream just because that lying asshole George didn't have your back like you wanted? Like you expected.*

There was no answer. No rationalization. No further conscious thoughts about the equipment that he'd intended to be the ticket to transform his life's dreams into his life's work.

Nothing but an empty unknown upwelling. He had no answer, and even though he hadn't spent all the cash he'd received on machine bets, he was increasingly scared to log in to his bank account and see what the damage was.

His savings had been abundant, aided by Tiffany's life insurance that drove his balance into triple digits because the servicer didn't know she'd died by her own hand.

Not mine, Glenn thought as he stood up from the cracked vinyl and left behind a slick musky imprint. *Never my fault. It was never my job to keep her alive once she knew my truth. My desires.*

He kept his jittering hands inside his long sleeves, and each step back toward the cabin on the lake sent buzzing splinters through his shins, arches, and toe knuckles. Would they ever stop moving?

The slush underneath his feet gave way just before he crossed the threshold, and he fell flat on his ass on the porch. Tiffany's voice was somewhere behind him, following from the infernal casino.

Never should've brought that damn token here.

"Go away, you nagging bitch!" he screamed into the dusky winter wind. "You don't get to be here. You don't get to ruin my life anymore! *I* get to be the bitch now. You owe me happiness for once in your goddamn existence!"

Only the wind responded, and it almost knocked him over again.

Back inside, his pups were sleeping on the floor, silver chains on their necks tied to the mantle.

"Wake up, my lovelies. Your handler needs you."

The boys stirred, but as soon as they started moving, they started crying out. Wails and whines of pain as they crawled toward him. *Ah. Ahh. Aroo.* It might've been a cute chorus of squeals in the right play, but he backed away from them as they crawled to his feet. There was something uneasy and grating about how they were doing it. They approached him until he fell backward into what he thought was the recliner chair but felt much different.

When he looked up, he sat on the knee of a tall old man with lines like canyon crags through every centimeter of skin. The man cradled Glenn's shoulder with an ice-cold grip, and in his hands was a red catlinite pipe beset with four spectral blue orbs. In each, the burned but sizable remnants of the rest of his stash—one pile a wet, reddish brown and another sickly and pale paste. One a crumbling mash of yellow shatter. The last orb stained black with an ugly, screaming soot.

In front the chair, his three boys—Noodles, Beef, and Spot—were on the floor, each shaking, thick veins like fungus spores in their eyes, mouths sopping with white foam as their neck leashes tugged at each other's, all cowering below the sight of their handler being handled.

"You've been such a good boy, Glenn," the man said. His voice carried a deep, physical quality to it, as if the air of each word burrowed into his ears and clawed its way toward his temples and chest. "Don't worry about your pets. They'll be out of their misery when I eat your heart."

"Why . . ." He tried to speak, but the man summoned flames on the tips of each of his fingers beneath each burned sphere. All four filled with smoke, and the man forced the end of the red pipe into Glenn's mouth. Sensation faded away in all parts of his body except his throat and filling lungs, and he lay nestled against the specter, full submission, while the walls around him pulsed and shook with static.

"Just like a newborn pup. Yes, get your fill. It won't be long before you're inside me, and don't worry about your friends here. You'll be gone by the time they find their bodies in the cabin under your name. Don't they already look so ripe, so easy to the taking?"

The three masked boys lay still. Each breathing but passed out, the red Neoprene tongues of the dog masks hanging out from their mouths.

"Glenn, the boy in the blue mask, he's been stealing from you. I can see in your puppy-dog eyes that you bought his story, and naturally that leads you right to thinking maybe he's a keeper. Usually, I fill my patients' heads with dreams, but I should pull you from your fairy tale before you fall in. He has four children with two different women, and several family members have restraining orders. Just a violent one, that boy is. Rabid dog in a puppy mask. It's okay, Glenn. All monstrous mutts started with closed eyes and whimpers; we needn't fault ourselves when we can't see the transformation.

"The day I found you is as lost to your memory as it is of mine, but I'm certain the day after you proposed to the lovely girl in the waterslide. But she was always temporary, wasn't she? Your fate was always to grow for me, Glenn. Grow me another pair of eyes alongside a thick-skinned heart of the northland with a craving for the flesh of man. You've had your sweets, and now I'll have mine."

The figure's wretched eyes split into hundreds, thousands of pairs, and with them, centuries of stories, all peering at him at once.

There was a warrior of old. On the island where the seashell brought our people, he lived in a golden land where nobody starved. But his hunger was not for the bountiful food of that burgeoning Pillager empire. It was for the power of healing that had saved several of the men in his family in the aftermath of west-men battles. He approached manhood and sought their help.

What he found were lecherous sorcerers, driven mad by starlight power. They were feasting on the young in the dark of night, and the boy, trained warrior as he was, fought to put an end to their vile lodge.

To defeat the men's vile witchcraft, the boy prayed to the spirits of his mothers and grandmothers, but to his shock, their fires did not burn. The boy overcame and collected the men's faces and scalps for his own, though they added much weight as he traveled.

But even with their lodge destroyed, the boy's work was in vain, for the spark of civilization that built the land had already festered. No sacred city lasts forever, and soon every goddamned wigwam was burned or thrown in the great waters, and with them, they hoped, the memory of those atrocious days. And whenever that boy saw his face in the reflection of a lake, he wept and he wailed as the men laughed back. That old-time Indian humor you hear about.

These memories live on, Glenn. Why don't you give them a look? Tell me if I told the story wrong.

Glenn felt the man's fingers trace the ridge above his brow, and he screamed so loud it shook the pups awake.

Then all at once, his vision became a fast-spinning void.

*

When he came to, the old man who'd been cradling him still had him by the neck, but now a fierce chain saw growl erupted from a flappy throat, and his face had a hundred furious eyes laser-locked on a shape in the doorway on the far side of the cabin.

Glenn moaned through the lanky fingers still lodged in his neck, and hope filled every nerve in his body.

Puck, the boy from Atlantis, stood at the entrance, a crooked smirk spread wide underneath an icy glare. Behind him the wall still moved and his field of vision in general was splotched and fuzzy, so the boy's gaze was overcast with a blood-crimson swirl. "What hempen homespuns have we wagering here?"

A harsh and clawing gasp of breath forced its way through the lump in Glenn's throat, and his breathing returned to normal. The claws in his neck fell away, and the man screamed.

"What the hell are you pretending to be in that costume?" Puck said.

Another guttural explosion from the old man's warping, spasmodic face.

"Oh, I'm sorry. *Regalia*," Puck sneered. "Bet you'll do great in the fancy dance contest."

There is no worth to the words of a creature whose ancestors I've eaten.

"Most animals have mouths. No one's impressed that someone taught you to chew."

The old man dropped Glenn to the floor and lunged toward Puck but stopped just as quick. In Puck's hands, faster than Glenn's eyes could see, was a small wooden bow, nocked with an arrow that pulsed with writhing yellow lights on the fletchings.

Just then, the cabin lamp's dun glow seemed to double on his vision, as if he'd fallen into a deep sleep and come to, but he'd felt no time pass or darkness fall between the time he saw the bow and when the demonic man fled the cabin.

"I think you might be partying a little too hard there, pup-per." Puck unbound the three men on the cabin floor from all their gear, and when he ran his fingers across their foreheads, an x in charcoal appeared on each. All still very unconscious but breathing. Finally, Puck turned his full attention to Glenn and sighed, still looking not a day older than nineteen. "I can't keep him away from you forever. But if you get away from this land now, you might just have a chance to escape his net, little fish."

"I can't just leave," Glenn said, overcome by a torrent of panic, relief, fear, and despair. "Look at all this . . ."

"Hey now." Puck walked over and ran his fingers over the sides of Glenn's head through his remaining hair. "I might have a guy or two I could see about all this."

Glenn looked into the young man's eyes. The same young, naive, lustful face, still enticing now, with such smooth skin and eyes a deep ocher brown but now somehow shrouded in a mystery Glenn was not privy to.

"I never should've come back," Glenn said. "But whatever the hell you are and whatever possessed you to help me . . . thank you."

With that, he scrambled to his feet, threw on a quick layer of baggy clothes that he hoped would keep him warm in the winter night, and left the cabin in his rearview with the boy from the screen.

Chapter 17 PASSING THROUGH A PRAIRIE COUNTRY

MARION LAFOURNIER

First Day

The sky is a giant snowflake, filled with branching lines like a piece of shattered opal. It writhes and pulses in hexagonal waves as I open my eyes, and when the sleep is shaken away by the bitter cold, the display above fades away in a four-pointed star of soft, pale clouds. Four, then six, eight, and soon the sky looks soft and welcoming as a star quilt. Small, sharp flakes descend. I roll myself up.

In all directions, rows and rows of spiky, snow-covered grassland, crooked stalks of corn, the snaking shapes of slender trees—a desolate plain in deep winter. The soft indent of a long road.

The coat from the gas station sits heavy on my shoulders, still wet from the snow and the lake.

My fingers shake, panic or cold or both, and I scan the ground around my feet. No sign of grass, gravel, or earth. Just a compact land of crunched snow.

On either side, the frozen grass moves in a whiplike motion. The slender trees roll and crumple and dance, in and out of sight. The corn fades from pale gold to oily green and black, rotting in and out as the leaves of the stalk wither into purple fists, erratically swatting at the snowflakes on the air.

Far in the distance, towering above everyone, a silhouette is just visible through the storm, a giant mountain with pale blue ridges and spires.

"No."

I dig my fingertips into my forehead and smack my face over and over.

"No. No, that's not what happened."

My feet sink into the snow, the compact crunch suddenly soft powder. It welcomes me like loose sand might.

"I'm not dead," I cry out. "I'm on the lake. The lake. Shannon will be here soon. I—ah. Ah."

But the sky itself, the jagged lines of ice clouds spell it out for me so well. Shimmering with purple and green brilliance. *You died.*

I double over, and my bare hands sink into the churning snow.

"*Bazigwiin! Azhigwa.*"

My body understands and follows the command before my mind can understand it consciously. *Stand up! Now.*

On my feet, I can see where the voice came from. Hovering at eye height, an impish creature in a slick feathered cloak watches me with wide, curious eyes.

No bigger than a human toddler, the being has a squat, furry head, with a pointy tuft of hair in the middle, like an onion. On either side of the tuft, two cream-colored horns arc out, pointing at each other in two crescents. Its eyes are wide, catlike, but with a pointed nose I mistake for an owl's beak. Sticking out of its short snoutlike mouth, two small teeth curve opposite its horns.

Flipper-like feet stick out from the bottom of its feather

cloak, on which a pattern of dappled white over deep brown and beige tells me its cloak is made of loon.

Around its neck is a string of sinew that held a wooden circle with an equal-armed cross burned into it. The pendant looks like a colorless medicine wheel, but the lack of color somehow makes it look more sacred.

"*Hay'sa*," the creature says. "A boy greets fate and mourns for it. And me without some food."

My voice is caught between *who* and *what*, and I gawk at him until he laughs, a trill, owllike hoot.

"My name, my name? Little Loon gets asked his name by the Nameless Boy." He floats closer to me until his face is inches from mine, grabbing my forehead, inspecting me with eyes and nostrils. For a moment he sounds more bulldog than whatever birdy creature he is.

"I smell the Anishinaabe blood in you, Nameless. Coming to this land, proof enough, yes. And some evil ones pretend to be human and they lie. But Little Loon's senses don't."

"Little Loon? Okay. What are you, Little Loon?"

"Your ancestors called us *Memegwesiwag*. The Little Butterfly People."

"Oh." I surprise myself with the amount of the delight in my quivering voice. "I've heard a lot of . . . other people's stories about you."

"Good things all, yes, yes? Bad things none, at least that I've done." He holds out two raccoon-like paws from under the feathered shawl. "These hands are for guidance, not nuisance." A wide smile of tall, pointy teeth spreads. "They can choose nuisance, though."

"Where am I, Little Loon?"

"Hasn't your *Mishomis* taught you?"

"Er. No, I didn't really grow up with a grandfather."

"Why not?"

"Men die young on the reservation."

A wrinkle comes across his face. He uses his flippery foot to scratch at what I can only assume are hidden short ears near the base of his horns. "*Bekaa, bekaa, bekaa!* There are mysteries of your walking world, Nameless, that I can't understand."

"Like a reservation?"

His head flutters, and he dips his head to rub his cheek against his shoulder blade. "There was once so much Anishinaabe land across the great turtle's back. Golden light all over for us spirits to walk alongside our younger brothers, the men. But those lights are but a scattering of stars on a dark turtle shell. These little lights. Is that what you speak?"

I give myself a quick mind visual of what he said and then nod back. "Yes. And sometimes those lights take our people too young."

"Don't I know it, Nameless Boy. I've greeted them before bringing them to the mountain." He points at the massive silhouette in the distance. "The Fourth Hill awaits all."

I sigh when he says the phrase. Our stories tell us we walk four great hills, each a season, and the final one is an endless winter. One whose other side is probably the greatest mystery. "So I did die."

He places a small finger under my chin. "Gaawiin. You're standing in front of me. You didn't come to this land as others do. I pulled you in."

I remember the outline of the door on the rock and those little hands on my shoulders. "That was you. You saved me from the sandman."

The dwarf spirit's eyes deepen into a coal black, and at first it seems intimidating, but eventually he reminds me of a mouse. "Yes, yes, you're here because of me, but I know nothing of sand. But the False Eldest. Oh, I know his scent."

"So why save me from him?"

The dwarf spirit drifts to the ground, his light feet staying on top of the ice like snowshoes. "All creatures under the Up Above have a role, and mine is for the younger siblings. I bring their souls to the mountain."

I take a step back. "Are you going to try to get me to the mountain?"

"No other way back. If you *want* to go back. Up to Nameless."

"It's okay, Little Loon. You can call me Marion."

"Follow me, Nameless."

Without a further word, Little Loon skips across the snowy road, expecting me to follow. He doesn't turn back for what feels like a mile, but in this cold weather—and now my boots soaked completely through—it could've been a lot less.

Out of breath and shivering out of control, I stop and rest with my hands on my knees. Beneath my feet, the snow churns again, this time burying my legs to the knee.

"Always best to keep moving on this road, Nameless."

"Why do you keep calling me that?"

"All warriors need a name the Creator recognizes in our sacred language." He finally turns around and flutters back to me. "But when I try to know yours, all I see is an empty spot that's waiting for a name. Are you looking for a name in your world?"

The glowering nickel eyes of the plastic shaman flash in my head. "Carey. That's right. I never went back. He never got a chance to—to dream and bless me with the name."

"Oohn," the dwarf says. "So there is still something netting you to the world of men. I can sense it out there, lost and waiting for a Nameless Boy."

"I hope so."

"Your legs still aren't moving, Nameless."

"Sorry, sorry." I dig my numb legs from the churn and continue on the road. "It's just so cold. I wish my clothes hadn't gotten soaked."

"If you want warmth," Little Loon said, "you'll have to earn it." He pulled out a small wooden bow and a quiver full of tiny arrows, no bigger than a ballpoint pen. "Shoot the snow in the eye and conquer the cold."

I grab the bow, which is smaller than the full length of my already-petite-for-a-man hands and nock one of the pencil arrows. The arrowhead bursts into flames when I pull the string, and when I release, it sputters away into the ugly prairie grass.

"Ope. You'll have to try again."

"How many tries do I get?"

"It's a little people bow, as one of your *other people's* stories might say." The dwarf cackles. "Many, many as you like."

I notch another, and again the tiny end of the arrow bursts into flame like a matchstick. "Can't I just use the arrows to warm up?"

"Lazy warriors get stuck among the stars, Nameless. If you can't weather this storm, the land will claim your body before the snow covers it all."

I take a deep breath, nock, and shoot another, this time a little higher in the air.

"Shoot, miss. Shoot, miss," Little Loon says. "All the time you need."

I launch several more, but all of them fizzle away like bottle rockets, and not that I can see, but it looks like none shoot any snowflakes in the eye.

I crane my neck straight upward, and sure enough, I see

the shape of a giant cloud of jagged ice lines, an ever-morphing snowflake. I nock the bow and shoot straight into the air.

The crystal shatters, and in a matter of moments, all of the snow disperses on the ground. The land and sky are clear.

"A very sturdy bow," he says. "Time to go."

The snow no longer churns when I stand still because in the distance the clear image and immense size of the Fourth Hill demand my body stop and my eyes transfix on the sheer majesty of the mountain. The last place our souls could ever visit. The Fourth Hill of Winter, taller, wider than the idea of a sky itself.

Chapter 18 ☠ DREAMCATCHER WITHIN A DREAM

ALANA BULLHEAD

February 21, 2018

Every now and then as the weeks passed, when she found herself back in Geshig where she and Cherie had spent their childhood days, they wouldn't answer the door at the detox center.

"Where's my sister? She's been sick."

"She's not here, ma'am. You know this. Please leave the premises, or we'll be forced to call the tribal cops to escort you again."

So it went, on and on, until she learned to stay away.

Instead, she wandered in the sleepy web of hallways through all her favorite casinos. All the way in North Dakota, where this casino held a short-order grill in the same room as the roulette tables. Where the VR headsets in the poker galley purported a hybrid form of battlefield stud.

On the *Lucky Lotus Leaves* machine, she found herself staring at the intricate artwork of each billowing flower whenever they appeared on the reels. They were so soft, as if the screen were a canvas, and the petals rustled whenever the reels came to a halt. It was a newer machine, far more luxurious than the best of the best at her old job.

Leaving Atlantis after all those years should have pained her more than she currently felt. It was as easy to walk away from there once Cherie was gone as it was to switch from the lotus machine to the one across the row, *Golden Temple of Mystery*. A cubic palace of lined gold with splotchy green shrubbery falling out of its vaulted entrances, with the bonus tile a depiction of a brown marmoset hanging on a branch. Whenever free spins initiated, the marmoset squares flashed red and the marmosets jumped up and down manically.

In the bathroom of the casino, Alana hunkered on the toilet and took out five Percocets from underneath her bulky phone case.

*

Underneath a starless autumn night, in a cemetery so old the wooden planks of the grave houses looked like pillars of salt and pepper held together with thin, black wires, Alana dug into the ground with a spade shovel. The soil was already cold and chalky, but it wasn't far down where she'd buried the leather pouch.

She'd been eleven years old when her aunt Elise had presented her with the bag made of deerskin hide with a puckered seam like a small moccasin and a silver snap holding the pouch shut. It had sixteen round, wooden beads, painted in medicine wheel colors, across the six strands of leather that fell from each corner and two from the center like chiffon. On the front of the pouch, beneath the snap and cover flap, a circlet of rougher hide, also painted like the typical medicine wheel, held tight against the bag from the center two strands woven through.

That's what it looked like in her mind's eye and memory,

clearer than anything that had happened to her in the past year, but what she found was a soil-caked mess that fell apart upon delicate inspect. A useless hope. She could not remember what had been in it when her aunt Elise had asked her to burn it on her sixteenth birthday, but whatever it was, it had awakened her sevenfire sight.

But now that world felt so alien to her that she couldn't slice through the fog and name the mystery.

Neon lights were her answer. Through a hazy casino floor with air so dry and ghost-stale she coughed bank after bank was a tall red machine, like an old pinball machine. A bright-red demon's face, with seven glowering orange orbs surrounding each pupil, which held even smaller bright vibrant green dollar signs. The slot machine named *seven Fire sights*.

When she played a mere dollar, a screen full of crimson, flame-wisped trios of *7-7-7*. Such a classic casino image. They connected in a web of neon-pink and yellow lines across the reels, like a map of a city bus or subway route, and the siren song declared her a Big Winner.

On the wall, the clock pointed midnight.

When she woke, the fragments of the bag that had once held her umbilical cord were gone, and she was in a hotel bed alone, all the way in Madison, Wisconsin, the memories of getting there fragmenting quicker than the bag in her dream.

*

On the first day of February, now three months since she woke to the news of her uncle's still-unsolved murder, Alana sat alone in a casino restaurant in Wolf Point, Montana, with a mushroom and Swiss burger basket with fresh kettle chips.

She couldn't bring herself to let the day pass without a

commemoration of him, but she couldn't do it around family or she might get herself caught in the sandman's jagged beadwork.

When she finished the quiet dinner in honor of the fallen Froglegs, she walked through the halls of the unfamiliar casino in Wolf Point, the more familiar mazes of slot banks, the bright yellow and bronze of the foil-painted plastic and the goldleaf wallpaper surrounding so many elderly gamblers. Another successful reservation business. She could drive in most directions across the country for hours, and all roads could lead her to the games.

The warmth, the clouds of smoke, the sounds of music, electronic, plucky, and tinny. A twenty-first-century heaven for those with torrents of cash in their sunset years, or not very much cash at all. Still, they gathered for the rewards of grandeur.

A giant jackpot here. Winning scratch-offs and pull tabs there.

Blackout midnight bingo, where all the numbers gave one lucky patron ten thousand beautiful dollars when the sky was black and starless but the casino hall was softly lit with greasy yellow lamps.

A luxurious lifestyle, waiting just beyond the click of buttons, drawing of cards, sheets bespattered with inky circles in an almost neat calico. Tabs pulled, chips bet, coins dropped into thin, red, plastic caverns, never to be seen again.

She walked through a fresh cloud of some elderly patron's cigarette smoke and recalled the voices at Cherie's funeral, a Christian hymn in Ojibwe, listed in her book as "There Is a Land That Is Fairer Than Day."

In the sweet by and by
We shall meet on that beautiful shore

She looked around and saw the casino as that shore, a lost, ephemeral city where every cloud shone with the light of paradise, lovely in all affect, warm and welcoming.

> *We shall meet, we shall sing, we shall reign,*
> *In the land where the saved never die;*
> *We shall rest free from sorrow and pain,*
> *Safe at home in the sweet by and by.*

No, Alana thought. *This golden palace of misery is not our hereafter.*

Though many of their people sang of gods and prophets from an ocean away at their funerals, the Ojibwe were always a northern people who traveled at the mercy of Gichigaming, coldest, largest lake on Turtle Island. They were cold-water women and men. Deaths did not lead into the warmth of golden clouds, of harps and plucky music, of opulence or sedentary peace.

The Ojibwe walked the winter.

Alana stepped out of the casino's front door and stared across the flat, cold, and desolate Montana prairie.

Her great-aunt Elise's words to her the first time she attended a funeral and saw the family member's feet pointing west:

To the Ojibwe, our destiny lies to the west. Death is passing through a prairie country.

A gust of razor-sharp wind blasted her face and flooded her eyes with tears. She covered her eyes with her palms to wipe away the burning moisture, but when she removed her hands, it was some other prairie she saw. One underneath a murky green atmosphere.

And her cousin, Marion, wandering through deep snow, shivering like a startled rabbit.

She shouted for him. The wind suppressed the volume, but for just a moment, he turned in her direction. Far ahead of him, the prairie turned to a flat expanse of ice, slowly fracturing and revealing a placid, black lake underneath, its breath as cold as hibernating catfish.

Then she was back at the casino, her eyes burning bright red and filling her with a clear light she hadn't known since before she lost the baby.

Seven fires in her eyes.

Just as quick as it came back, it faded away, and she cried tears of joy. If it could come back for a brief moment, she could bring it back again. She just needed the right fire.

*

After a soak in the hotel's hot tub and then a long sweat in the sauna, Alana went back to her room. In her bed was a replacement body for Zach, an unassuming paramour who was napping while she gambled. He stirred as soon as she walked in. Simon was another slim white man, but this one covered in tattoos of his favorite cartoon characters, plants, and molecules. Truthfully, it was that self-branding of the molecules that attracted her; he was an inked-and-slammed-up man, the exact type needed when she'd drifted out of her life and needed to forget the waking nightmare.

Alana scanned the room for a usable organic material, her first choice being a fancy lamp made out of some twisted driftwood. When she broke a few branch segments off, Simon finally woke, sat up, and focused his sleepy attention on her.

"Morning, babe."

She paused, staring at his frame, at his physical presence,

this replacement who could be no more than passing fancy and a plug.

"You trust me, right?" Alana asked.

"Like with cash? Stash? Or . . . ?"

"Just in general."

"Yeah, sure." He giggled and stretched out his arms with a high-pitched, canine groan. "You haven't left me yet."

"Good. Because I'm going to do something that might not make sense to you now. But I need you to let me do it. And if you do, if you can stand it, maybe I'll help you out too."

He tilted his head in confusion as she piled a stack of matches in a glass ashtray and lit them on fire. Slowly, their trails spread to the pieces of the driftwood lamp, and when embers were glowing, she picked them up with her fingertips. They burned, but only a fraction of pain compared to what would come next.

"If it doesn't work," she said to Simon the replacement, "I want you to know it's not your fault."

She opened her eyes wide and stuck the glowing embers onto her corneas.

Alana's screams overpowered his, but she held the embers in place long enough before he jumped and ripped them from her hands. At first, he tried to cradle her. Then he paced around the room, screaming about getting caught after a hospital visit.

"No need," she said, taking her hands away from her face and looking at him. Trails of blood fell from her eyes, and no doubt there was damage she'd need tended to. But something more beautiful than she could imagine wavered around her replacement's frame: a glowing aura, mostly blue-tinged with the ugly purple and green fumes of their shared chemicals. If she looked in the mirror, she would certainly see her own.

But to *see* again, to regain the blessing of the seventh prophet . . .

That was worth more to her than all the manmade chemicals on Turtle Island.

*

When she woke the next morning, the newspaper in the hotel room read February 25, 2018. The replacement man was still in her bed, but she could see in the air around the room, clearer with each minute, the sinewy threads of this fell dreamcatcher's trap. Every weave and stitch she could see shimmering through the air.

Alana left the room behind and rushed to the casino floor. She must physically still be in Montana, that much felt clear and tangible, but the date meant returning to Geshig would still deliver her to a headstone she wouldn't accept.

The sandman had taken her sight but not her life, and that would be his end. She smiled as she stood near the center of the casino floor and looked around.

There were no clocks on the walls.

Chapter 19 ☠ HOMEWARD ROAD

MARION LAFOURNIER

Second Day

Hours passed on the second day on the wintry road until the white sky faded to soft blue, deeper until nearly pitch black. Little Loon's feathered cloak shimmered a pale gray glow, and the dappled spots danced back and forth as he floated along.

"Can we make camp?" I shout to him over the wind.

He flutters back to me and laughs as he circles around, gliding as smooth as a loon diving for fish.

"It would be a mistake to make camp in this land."

"I don't think I can make it, Little Loon. My legs. My everything. Too cold."

He sighs. "Dangerous are all paths outside the Ojibwe's world, but you knocked on the door."

"It was a gamble. I thought that was the only way out."

"I hear that word a lot on this road. But never from the tongues of my kind who lived on the Creator's First World. What does it mean?"

"Taking a risk in hopes of cashing out. The sandman had me trapped, and Makwade said he knew of another road."

"Your aura doesn't speak of a warrior who acts foolish."

"Little Loon, if I had an aura, it wouldn't be a warrior. You're not hearing that speak because it's not there."

"The Four-Day Road is not a river to use at your convenience, child."

"Like I said, it was a gamble. I couldn't know what would happen, not like Alana does."

"Ah, ah, eh, what is it your cousin thinks she sees? Is she one of the profound nappers?"

"She said she has sevenfire sight."

The little round spirit shakes with laughter. "Sometimes a napper is just a napper and a napper who dreams is still just a man in tribe with no job to do."

"She has a job, though. She works at Hidden Atlantis."

"I don't know this Atlantis, or any of those shiny places many of my charges come from. But I've caught the scent of it on their auras, and it reeks of snake scales and unnatural fire."

"That's true. But that's where she worked. I remember that much."

Little Loon keeps silent and lets the whipping hiss of the prairie take his place. He floats behind me and nudges my shoulder.

"I can't keep you walking each time, Nameless. I can only guide you along—oh, oh, oh, another traveler?"

The feathered dwarf leaps down, the tips of his doll-like feet resting just above the snow. He looks back to me and smiles. "*Ambe!*"

My legs pick up their pace at his command.

Not far off the trail, beyond a copse of prickly grass and old corn stalks, Little Loon stops. Ahead, across a small river, a young woman with a black ponytail sits on a blanket with a bundled baby.

I shake my head and brush away a tear with my soaked

jacket sleeves. "This is one of his nightmares, right? One of his games."

"It's okay, Marion," Cherie says. A voice that feels layered with an unceasing happiness, one of motherly love and content, of friends, and of promises. "Grand entry gotta keep circlin'. Guests gotta keep walkin' the floor. You may not have gotten to know me well in your life, but then, I didn't get to know you much when I was alive. Can't always play on the same bank. Sometimes there's just more room for others."

The baby coos.

"So small, but it's okay."

Little Loon cradles the bundle in his right arm and leans his forehead against Cherie's cheek. "I can help you both, if you want to follow me."

I try to hold back tears as the snow subsides. From behind Cherie and Alana's baby, a pale but faintly green light shines.

"I've never seen it before," Little Loon says, voice soft as a red leaf in autumn. "But I've heard a lot of my travelers talk about springtime somewhere beyond that hill. Do you two want to leave now?"

"Can I think it over? Right now, I need to help my little godson get his rest. I even have a dreamcatcher for him." She brings up a black-and-silver-blue spiderweb around a teardrop circle of ash branch. "I've always loved that I can use dreamcatchers without feeling all tacky. Know what I mean, Marion? *Neh*."

"Was it the sandman?"

"Ah, none of that matters now. You just keep doin' whatever you're doing, and I'll take care of this boy here."

I can barely get the words out when my voice cracks. "I'm sorry we never spent much time together in life."

Cherie shrugs. "Eh. Don't worry about it. Happens when you got a big family."

Little Loon floats to my shoulder and leads me away from the river with his small, furry hand. "You could stay with them if you want, Nameless. That's what this land is here for."

"But I promised Alana . . ."

"*Hay'sa*," Little Loon says. "Promise made; debt unpaid."

"So I need to get out. I need to get back to Atlantis and Alana."

"My boy, there's only one way out. You know that. It's always been there." He points in the distance at the towering hill of winter. "*Wajiw.* The final mountain."

I wipe the tears from my eyes and continue on the four-day road through the prairie.

Chapter 20 💀 NORTHERN LIGHTS, QUEER SIGHTS

MARION LAFOURNIER

Third Day

On the dawn of the third day, Little Loon dancing and shaking the whole way, I collapse near the first slope of the mountain. But the churning snow doesn't try to pull me under.

Instead, I hear a chorus of laughter from farther up on the hill, on a ridge of sapphire-blue rock not far above the first steep incline. Above, the rest of the hill blocks out the sky, dominion cast over all the land.

Seven shadows leap from the rock and approach.

The first to come into view is a towering moose wearing a coat of eagle feathers, followed by a great gray rabbit the size of a horse. It wears a necklace of foxtails and crawls on thick-clawed knuckles. Three look like otters, but with slippery-skinned faces and fur laced with shimmering scales. Like Little Loon's coat, it's hard to tell which part of their general shape is anatomy and which is wardrobe. A stork-like bird wanders into view, rather plain looking except for the veins of electricity that zip through its feathers now and then like a meteor shower. The last is a raccoon, also waddling, though closer to the size of a small bear.

They speak as one, but not with voices. The words aren't English or Ojibwe, but rather something old and ancient, humming out from all their bodies.

Who presumes to walk the mountain of eternal tribulation?

Little Loon answers for me.

"Old friends, elder brothers, I serve with honor, leading those who've left their bodies. But this young man has something of a dispute over his status."

The road of souls is not a barter.

"This one has been fighting the False Eldest."

The beings don't move, but all are filled with a pulse of anger that I can feel through my coat.

Speak your name, Nameless One.

"I go by Marion. But I'm not nameless like you think. Earlier this year a man promised to dream a name for me."

What spirit in your world gave him permission to dream of names?

"I don't know. I had to take him at his word."

Another pulse vibrations through my ears, this one like static. I can hear their whispers among each other, but none of it comes into my mind as intelligible.

Is the Nameless One a worthy warrior?

"I mean, I've never thought so."

"The boy follows," Little Loon says. "Not many follow the road of souls without the winter claiming their foolish hearts."

He must prove his honor.

As they speak their demand, their bodies slowly morph from big animal shapes to human but for masks of flames and starlight that hold back their faces. All but the thunderbird, who is unmasked and has the face of a young woman.

"What games do you know?" she asks.

I laugh and shrug. "Not many. I used to play some card games with my mother and grandma. Wisk, blackjack, war."

"War it shall be!" one of the taller beings says, his fists raised to the sky.

"Not that kind of war!" I shout quickly. "A card game."

"It's queer games where this boy come from," Little Loon says. "Nothing risky for their delicate skin."

War it shall be.

They speak as one again, with finality. The unmasked girl smiles, and a red crown of leaves appears in her hand when she reaches out to me. "A crown for the king of the harvest windigoog."

I place the crown on my head.

You will play three games, though you need only win one to leave. Failure means you will finish crossing the mountain.

"What are the rules?"

All seven beings and the dwarf cover their faces with their hands.

"First you hide," Little Loon says, peeking at me through the gaps in his feathered sleeve. "Then they look for you. When they get close, you can either hope they don't find you or run out to start the fight. If you beat the leader in a wrestle, you win. Mind your time, though. They won't wait forever." He covers the rest of his face with one arm and shoos me away with the other.

I back away and turn into a run in the opposite direction of the group. Not far into it, I look down and see my boots leaving deep footprints in the snow. The land around is jagged and rocky, but even without the foot trail, I'd bet that they could easily sense where I am.

But he said the point wasn't to hide well but to spar when found.

I find a copse of dried bushes near some rocks a half mile away from the beings and crouch behind it. I wait for the crunch of their feet.

Suddenly, the gray landscape around me is alight in deep green and red colors. I look up and see dancing aurora lights. They descend on the mountain like falling mist.

Minutes later, the padding footsteps approach but fade away in a few directions before circling back. When they seem close, I run out for the confrontation.

The being at the front of the line easily swats me away and then pins me down on my face with my arms crossed over my chest.

"You got lucky," Little Loon says. "Almost. Someone *Up There* must be really impressed by you to send the *waawaate* to hide you."

"Do I get more chances than this?" I say through the side of my mouth as the rest of my face is held firm against the snow.

"The King of the Harvest Windigoog has been defeated," bellows the voice who pinned me down. "You won't hunt our people anymore!"

"Okay, okay. So what's next?" The being lets me up, and then I ask it its name.

"In Ojibwe," the being says.

"*Aanii*—wait, you're not using the language! Neither is Little Loon."

More group laughter follows.

"All who lived in the First World knew every sound nature could make before the flood. All languages, all songs."

I scan my memory for the deluge she speaks of. In school we had so many speakers, so many textbooks, so many Ojibwe teachers who gave their own ideas of our people's history that it's hard to remember what's generally accepted as authentic.

I do remember a flood, just like Genesis. Actually, one of the white substitute teachers for Ojibwe class in high school suggested that the Ojibwe flood myth was a product of the Christian inquisition of America. I think he was reprimanded for that, but who knows if he was correct. Pretty sure every culture has a flood myth.

I retry asking the presumed leader of the beings his name. "*Aaniin ezhinikaazoyan?*"

"Bezhig."

In Ojibwe, One.

"Does that mean the rest of you are . . ." I close my eyes, trying to recall simple elementary school lessons. "Niizh. Niswi. Niiwan. Naanan. Ningodwaaswi?" They all nod once as I guess each of their names. All but the maskless spirit in the form of an Ojibwe woman.

"*Ishkode indizhiwiinz.*" My name is Fire.

"What's the next game?"

Bezhig answers, "Snow snake." In his hands, two wooden sticks appear, each about the size of an average forearm. Scorch-mark scales have been burned into the wood. "Whoever throws the farthest while keeping the snake above the snow wins."

Bezhig steps forward, hands me the snow snake, and then whips his in a helicopter motion in the distance. It flies for miles until out of sight.

A cold churn of water spins through my chest as it sinks in. They were never going to let me win, only humoring my request.

"So I lose," I say, dropping the stick in the snow.

"Perhaps not," Bezhig says. "If my snake sank under the snow without surfacing, I lose if yours stays up." He laughs. "You'll have to find it, though."

It feels like further mockery, but one last hope is the only thing ahead of me other than the farther side of the mountain. I toss my snow snake ahead of me just as he did, but it only slides about ten feet and stays on the snow.

"Guess we're doing this."

I walk in the direction where Bezhig threw his snow snake, and the spirits follow. Little Loon zips around like a hummingbird. "Don't underestimate this one," he chirps.

We walk in silence, the seconds turning to minutes or hours, my heels and toes so sore and taxed from the past four days of walking. The landscape blurs in and out of focus until all I can do to fight wind is cover most of my face.

"Don't look in the distance, child," Bezhig says. "Some sights in the winter lands can drive weaker men half mad."

The word *weaker* annoys me, so I reflexively turn in the direction he said not to.

At the edge of the white slope, the pristine snow turns to rotten black ice. The shape closest to the mountain is a ring of contorted old men, holes in their skin and chests as they rest in frozen agony.

"These are the graves of his victims," Ishkode says. "Until he accepts the four-day road, they cannot finish their mountain journeys."

Thousands more shapes are spread out across the expanse of black ice leading away from the mountain.

Just beyond the ring of old men is a giant, headless eagle half buried in the foul snow. The remaining stump of a neck is caked with rust-brown blood. The snow churns when my feet touch, but I keep walking. When I get closer, the eagle trembles and cowers. Even without a face I hear it plead with me for warmth.

The eagle envelopes my whole body with its wings and leans against me. I turn my face away from its neck but hold its embrace tight.

Tears fall across my cheeks and freeze in place. Even though it's headless, I remember this great beast. At the train tracks, a memory from when I was a toddler. Or maybe I just built the memory after hearing my mother talk about it so much. Whether it was real or not, I couldn't care less because there's no doubt in my mind this is the same sorrowful creature.

I take in a deep breath. "I have a new request," I shout back to Little Loon and the seven beings. "Instead of playing my final game, just free this one. Give my name to him so he can leave here. I'll stay on the mountain."

All eight voices behind me laugh.

"Nameless Boy, full of heart," Little Loon says.

One final game, the spirits say, once again in ethereal chorus.

When I turn around, the spirits have assembled a leather mat with four old moccasins on each end. In each of their hands is an array of instruments, drums, rattles, flutes. In between the two rows of moccasins is a pile of long sticks among a handful of round stone figures. Little Loon sits on the edge of the mat and smiles at me. "I'll be his partner."

"What the hell is this?"

"The moccasin game," Ishkode says. "The rules are simple."

She proceeds to describe a game that is not simple at all, and none of the rules stick in my head as she describes them.

"No."

All including Little Loon gape at me, some of the spirits angrier than others.

"This is your last chance," Bezhig says.

"I'm done with games of chance. You can all have fun here

gambling, I'm going to try to help this bird. Apparently, that's the one thing you all can't do."

I turn back to the eagle.

"I don't know if you can hear me without your head, but I remember you. I think you were calling out to me for help, but I was just a kid. But maybe I can save you from this nightmare now and take the pain away. Heh. It's funny because I didn't even really want an Ojibwe name. I just wanted some answers about Kayden and the wolf spirit that was following me. The offer of a dream name was a la carte, so you can have it. I don't know how this works or where the name even is, but it's yours."

Little Loon circles above us like a cherub. "Nameless Boy stays Nameless Boy. But do you know the name your guide dreamed for you?"

I shrug and throw my arms up in defeat. "Never looked into it afterward."

The voice of the seven spirits call in unison once again. *We know the name your* mide *dreamed, for we know all sounds nature can make. If this is your decision, we will grant it.*

Ishkode walks to the eagle and whispers something onto her wing. Electricity ripples across its giant feathers, and from the neck stump a great gray stone in the shape of an eagle head erupts. When it caws, the sky above turns into gray storms. The black ice that held its talons and feathers in place melts away, and the bird is freed.

All the spirits stare in awe, and the first one to break is Bezhig, who beelines to me and asks, "So are you finally brave enough to walk the mountain?"

The thunderbird's new stone head stares at the spirit. "No. He's not."

The thunderbird's talons grip the shoulders of my gas

station coat, and it launches into flight, high above the mountain, where the air grows colder than I've ever felt, but brighter and peaceful beyond words. The last thing I see on the mountain is Little Loon's wide, sharp smile.

Chapter 21 ☠ ICE AUGUR

ALANA BULLHEAD

February 28, 2018

If Marion truly was trapped in ice like her sight kept telling her all through the drive back to Minnesota, she would need to find him before going back through the silo.

She drove onto the Languille Lake Reservation, this time with four lines of charcoal on her face: on her forehead a sort-of rounded lowercase *b* with a dot above, a small circle on her right temple, one that looked like a lowercase *j* whose bottom curve was inverted, and on her chin a thick line in the shape of a horseshoe magnet.

In the Ojibwe syllabary, it read, in clockwise order, *Hide from him.*

One mile in, she dared hope it had worked. First time all year she'd been on the rez without hearing his fetid laughter somewhere on the wind. She used cash from the last thousand dollars of her savings to get a pixie cut and a big pair of blue sunglasses. If the stories held true, the charcoal should be enough to obstruct the *maji-manidoos*'s view of her face, but just in case some servant of his whose mortal eyes he controlled spotted her, she took an extra precaution.

Earlier in the day, she'd stopped at Zach's and asked if she could borrow his auger for ice fishing.

"Can't believe you'd think I'd trust you after months of cutting me off."

"You've every right to hate me, love."

"Don't call me that."

"It's important."

"I'm not gonna be responsible for you hurting yourself out on the ice." He crossed his arms. "Not that I care to stop you from trying."

She sighed, marveling at the distance between them. How easily persuading him used to come to her, but now he didn't know her from Skywoman.

Alana laced her fingers over her stomach. "I miss him. And I know you hate supernatural shit, but for once, please believe that I know what I'm talking about this time. Nothing can bring our son back, but I can bring pain to the ones who stole him."

She could tell by the hope that broke through his pit bull eyes and turned them back to puppies that it was what he needed to hear. What he'd wanted to hear the whole time.

"I don't wanna trust your promise." He sighed. "But do you promise?"

"I do." She brushed a lock of his hair out of his face, which had grown puffier and dryer since she last saw him. "Let me finish one last thing at the casino, and I'll be home."

"You don't work there anymore."

"Not yet. But someone must look out for it. Lot of Native kids out there who need jobs and could stand a little bit of work."

"A little bit of long work."

She laughed. It was something of a motto among the casino's employees. "Little bit of long work."

*

Through Geshig and headed south, Alana saw no sign of him in the town. Nothing looked all that different. The snow piled lower than in previous years, but still all was cast in white-brown slush, and the town was quiet. On the southwest corner of town, she stopped at her father's house. Her old man was already half shot at only a quarter past noon, but he welcomed her and, thankfully, knew better than to ask too many questions about where she'd been these past months.

"It's been hard, but I've kept your mama going. Auntie Lenna, though . . . she's inconsolable some days, and down most."

"Some days I don't believe it's real," she said, though it was a lie. Every day she knew it wasn't real, that it was only the fell design of a psychotic pretender. But the less her family knew, the less chance they'd find whatever danger Marion was currently in.

"How is Aunt Elise?"

"Not good, kiddo. You and Liam really broke her faith."

"So maybe not the best time to ask her to borrow her bow and arrow."

"You could try. You were her favorite niece."

"I have a favor to ask."

"Anything but money, my shy little apple."

"I need to use your truck . . . and if you can, I need you to sober up and visit Elise for me."

"Okay," he said, with a slurry sigh, handing her the keys without hesitation. "But what for?"

"Ice fishing."

"Lakes are good for it right now. Stay safe, kid."

She hugged him and then went outside, threw Zach's ice auger in the bed, and used a stick of lamp charcoal to mark the side of each door with a thin, encircled cross.

*

Waubajeeg was thirty miles south, and each one closer to Hidden Atlantis was a nerve-racking hell, but soon enough she passed by and drove onto Jackson Lane.

For the next twelve miles, no ghost or spirits approached her father's truck or dared to jump in. She saw them on the edges of the road, walking up and down the ditches, bodies all in some state of convulsing torture. Their auras glowed purple and green, but when she passed by, their only reaction was confusion. Not only was the charcoal on her face working for her, but it worked for the truck, enough to pass through their playground unbothered.

A few miles outside of Indian Hollow, she drove the truck onto the first lake, and as soon as the wheels hit the ice, she removed her glasses. Seeing the snow-blind surroundings with glass correctives wouldn't help her. Only the seventh fire could.

Three and a half lakes later, she sensed nothing. No aura trail, no gut feeling accompanied her memory of the vision. Her cousin was in danger, somewhere near an expanse of inky black water that filled her with dread of him catching an icy grave. But the where kept escaping her sight! Her recollection was as formless and churning as those cold waves.

It took the rest of the evening and until well past noon the next day for her search to produce results, many of those hours spent huddling inside the truck for warmth after long walks across the ice. The weather had been kind, no snow or cloud cover, but the wind still blew harder across the open breaks in between the trees.

At night, she found a motel in Indian Hollow and kept to herself. The boundary's effect was instant when she passed through, and her sight was stifled from even the smallest of auras. She was glad to be out and searching again at the first sign of sunlight.

On Lake 35, southwest of Indian Hollow, Alana found the right sign.

A reddish-black fog billowed in and out of sight from a rocky grotto just beyond the lake shore. On the largest of boulders, the gold outline of a door, shrinking and expanding. Behind it, she could sense but not see a cold, infinite darkness that held the shape of an intersecting zigzag road.

Alana had only heard about doors like this, never seen one with her own eyes; in her part of the reservation, all openings to the spirit world were said to be buried deep underground, where children couldn't follow the little people. All the aunties argued about who was more right about the river dwarfs, but most agreed it was a bad idea to follow them. A child's mistake, for the frivolity of chasing a butterfly could send a distracted boy into the maw of danger.

A dark silhouette of a man walked through the door's aura and plunged downward.

She sighed and shook her head. "Must've followed the little people right through. Rookie mistake, cousin."

Alana jumped onto the roof of the truck and scanned the lake. Nothing visible to note on or around the lake, just more tree line and a few patches where snow had blown away in the wind and revealed the opaque surface. Tall, bushy stalks of grass poked through in a few small patches, dry and brown.

When the auger's drill broke through the ice, her attention returned to her body, now almost a mile from the grotto. Crystalline water gushed out from where shed drilled. She repeated the action four more times in a close circle, until the round ice walls gave way and a gaping icy maw stared back at her. She threw the auger and her purse away from the hole and took a deep breath.

The plunge stabbed at every inch of her skin when she jumped in. But the fire in her eyes helped her focus on warmth and regain control of her convulsing body, and in all directions, she saw a tranquil lake bottom and billowing lines of undisturbed sand like a new planet. In the darkness, the gleaming scales of a swirling shoal of fish.

Not just any fish, but a frenzy of big green bullheads. They parted when she approached, settling nearby with their lidless eyes on her and, in their place, Marion.

She could sense how it happened now. Marion's spirit, pulled through the threshold by the *memegwesi*, and the sandman casting his now-useless body out onto the lake like a rag doll.

The fish frantically gathering to break the ice and pull him under.

He was floating vertically, no movement that she could see from his chest or mouth, but his eyes opened when she grabbed his shoulder. At first, he was frantic and flailed his arms, but she avoided his swatting limbs, grasped his jacket firmly, and pulled him toward the light of the shattered surface. In the corner of her eyes, still so tender from the fire, she thought she saw the black-and-white-spotted shape of a loon dart away.

When they were both out of the water and on the thicker ice, she grabbed the stick of charcoal out of her purse. Her hands shook madly, but she managed to trace the four syllabic glyphs on his face like her own.

"I'll be right back!" she said. "I won't abandon you. I'm just getting the truck."

She ran back to her father's truck and drove as close as she dared to the broken surface. She blasted the heat and helped a despondent and shivering Marion stumble into the cab.

He attempted to speak several times until he managed the sounds. "Your face."

She looked in the mirror and saw the glyphs had faded with the water. She retraced them, hoping they hadn't been smeared long enough to call him. The deep red spider fissures on her corneas from the embers were brighter and bigger, the pain coming to her only now, after the frigid swim was sending her whole head into a thick and swelling migraine.

In the future she would probably need some sort of surgery, but for now her only concern was the sandman. And Marion.

"For what it's worth, I regret asking you to take him on. I should've just let you leave when you were still trying."

Marion shivered, but through it she could hear him laugh. "That wasn't your choice. Or mine."

"I could've asked someone else."

"No. He was never gonna let me leave. Not in this life, not in the winter." He leaned against the dash, holding the dry sweater over himself and the hot air vents like a tent.

"How the hell did my body survive under there?"

"It was the bullheads." Alana smiled and wiped a tear from her eyes. "Your clan will always help you through the cold."

Marion laughed. "Promises made. Debts unpaid." His voice trailed off under his breath before he looked up again.

"I promised to help. And I did. I know how you're gonna defeat him."

"How?"

Marion let the dry sweater fall behind him as he reached into his coat pocket. "Do you have a bow?" In his hands were three thunderbird feathers.

"No. But I know someone who does."

Chapter 22   A SANDMAN AND A SILO

MARION LAFOURNIER

February 28, 2018

Overhead, the thunderbird circles as Alana drives us away from the lake. I'm still shivering and feel like no amount of warmth will ever break the mountain's chill through my body, but Alana implores me to tell her everything I remember.

"You never follow the little people," Alana says. "Didn't one of our aunties ever tell you that?"

"I don't remember anything specific. I knew I should've been cautious, but there was nothing else to do but walk."

"You saw all seven of the fire prophets?"

"I don't know who they were, but there were seven of them."

"Did they tell you their names?"

"Uh. Yeah. One through six in Ojibwe, and then Fire."

Alana purses her lips and shakes her head. "When I was a girl, I was always told that winter was the shape of the land of death, but it's only a one-way street. No one can turn back."

"I didn't turn back, though. The thunderbird flew me up."

"And he left you in the lake."

"Well, who among spirits is perfect?"

"Certainly not the sandman."

"Pretender," I say. "He's no sandman. He's not a spirit. He was the youngest of the medicine men on the old Ojibwe capital. He stole their life spans. They called him the False Eldest."

Tears fall from Alana's eyes. "Well, if you can come back from the Fourth Hill, then maybe Cherie can too."

I try to push down the urge to inquire, but it fails. "How did she die?"

"The coroner says she overdosed, but I know she didn't relapse. I *know* she wouldn't have. The sandman stole her and my child from me. But when this is over, I know I can find her."

I bow my shivering head. "Time to make this over then."

Alana brings me to her father's house near Geshig. He welcomes us in and puts on a pot of lemon-ginger tea. I take a deep swig of the spicy, sweet water, and since I first left the casino, it's the first time I've felt warm.

Her father, Bruce, starts small talk with us in a gentle voice, and it seems as if there's an agreement between them to keep the chat as benign as possible. He asks me about my side of the family.

"My mother is Hazel Lafournier. She grew up around here and the cities. Her mom was Eunice Lafournier."

"Ah. That makes you Alana's second cousin on her ma's side. Bullhead's her great-great-grandmother."

"And my great-grandmother," I say. There's a vague recollection of the shoal of fish surrounding me in the lake that Alana described. "I've a feeling she's still looking out for the family."

Alana walks into another room and comes back with a long, gray suitcase.

"Could you excuse us, Dad?"

He nods and leaves the room. She drops the heavy case onto the couch and finishes her tea. When she opens it, there is a sleek black bow that looks like carbon fiber. Alana takes it out of the foam padding, sets it aside, and then takes off the foam layer. Hidden underneath is a tan bow so small it looks like a child's art project. "Guess the last thing to decide is how quick we wanna do this. Wouldn't blame you if you wanted to rest, but . . ."

"No." I finish my tea and stare at the date on the newspaper on her father's coffee table. February 28, 2018. Months since I first tried to move from Geshig and got caught in the sandman's viscous web. A barrage of unpleasant thoughts fill my head. Was I reported missing? Has my family been worried? I told my mother before I started all this not to worry, but it's been a year. "We either end it today or we lose today."

"That's what I hoped you'd say."

*

After a quick shower, careful not to let the charcoal glyphs on my face wash away, and a cycle of my gas station clothes in the dryer, I leave Bruce's house and walk north toward the center of Geshig.

After a few blocks of plain housing and boarded-up reservation cracker-box neighborhoods, I wait for a train to pass by and then cross the tracks. It's near the same crossing where I first saw the thunderbird as a child.

Past Main Street a few blocks, the elementary school and the big log cabin playground come into view. It's a Saturday, so no children are around, but a few teens are playing basketball at the hoops. They pay no attention to me as I pass by and head for the painted silo.

In the truck, Alana referred to this old building as Geshig's sacred silent guardian. Apparently, every small town that hasn't died yet keeps one around to house some sort of collective lifeforce, an energy that binds a community together.

In the field between the silo and the playground is the empty space where a merry-go-round used to be.

On one of the silo's octagonal faces, some artist has painted a depiction of the sandman and the thunderbird's head. The sandman's eyes are wide, his mouth agape, as if staring into the cosmos stoned. The bird's eyes stare up at him in a pitiful expression.

Where is my body, master? it seems to say. *This is no kind of life.*

Two thin planks of wood seal the door on the north side of the octagonal silo. But the wood is so old and tattered that both come off easily with a couple of soft tugs.

Dozens of black-and-gray spiders scatter across the chipped paint walls. I catch my breath for a moment before I exhale and laugh. Our house on the lake was covered in huge leggy beasties that make these ones look like plastic Halloween decorations. Once when was I was sitting on our back porch, a sizable wolf spider decided the shortest path to his nest was straight down my left shoulder and arm.

I thought that moment had prepared me better to deal with arachnids, but when I open the door and see the fog of webs, my left arm shudders at the memory of that day.

Alana said the only way to end his grotesque dreamcatcher was to unthread it dream by dream, nightmare by nightmare.

Before we left her father's house she added a few more glyphs to my face near the cloaking ones. She insists it says *friend to spiders.*

Inside the webs, what looked like the wrapped, hollow

carapaces and chitins are now an array of frenzied dewdrops, glowering in gentle blues and fetid greens.

I pull a blue mask tight across my face and take a deep breath. My left arm spasms one last time before I rush into the silo.

All at once, my senses are overwhelmed by the musty, soul smell of this spider haven, the dreams burning against my eyelids, as if someone were holding a flashlight a centimeter from my face. A few small spiders crawl under my mask and make circles across my face.

I resist the urge to scream as a group gathers on my right temple.

Friend to spiders.

I hear a million chittering whispers, not in words I comprehend but ones I feel in my ears. My breath escapes in a shaking sigh. Uncomfortably relieved.

"Where's the sacred guardian?" I ask.

For the first time, I'm able to focus on the rest of my body and surroundings. There's no ground beneath my feet, and even though my eyes are shut, I can feel a cavernous dark all around and beneath the pull of the silk.

The manidookaazo *ate him.*

"I need to kill him."

The chitters turn into a rhythmic storm as the spiders circle around me. I open my eyes. They're swirling upward like a cyclone, skating past all the glittering dreams and nightmares.

Climb.

I flail my arms and legs. There's nothing to grab on to. All the silk snaps and stretches beneath my palms and feet.

My hand wraps around one of the lights, a dark green oval with purple vines across its surface. There are heinous screams, wails of unending pain, and the head that dreamed them is a witness. One of the last warriors on LaPointe, who didn't escape in time to miss the sandman's madness.

The weeping and wailing drove him so mad he ran into the water of Lake Superior, and the sandman unhinged his jaw like a giant walleye and stole a warrior's last nightmare.

The warrior walked away from LaPointe, dreamless, aimless. Spiritually skinned and quartered.

All the skin, the skin of men.

I hold down my retching stomach. His changing face, that amorphous look of a sagging old man. Remnants of memories of his victims hanging from his body like molting deer velvet.

The higher I climb, the more my body pulses with glorious and horrible scenes and a building, raging river of white-hot ambition. Waking dreams captured and used by him like a battery.

Near the top of the silo, one glowing golden dream, a young warrior, exudes an Adonis aura and posture, standing over a crowd of fearful Ojibwe families on a shore, sobbing loudly with joy.

I take off the mask and bite down on the chitinous dream until it crunches and crumbles beneath my teeth.

The spiders scatter downward, and in every space in between the spider-made silk, collapsing blue veins flicker into view, twine of the fell dreamcatcher Alana spoke of.

Somewhere high above, I hear the wretched, shrill siren of a dying eagle's caw. The planks of the silo's roof burst inward, and spindly fingers wrap around my neck. The splintered wood scratches my shoulders as he pulls me out into the light.

"There you are, you little muskrat. I couldn't see you for a while, but it looks like you've finally accepted your fate."

His face, once an innocent, unassuming old man at a slot machine, is a melted wreck, the texture of an old, gnarled knot on a tree infected by fungus.

It moves and bubbles like a hatching spider's egg.

"You should know by now, Nameless. In real life the spiritual shitheads don't offer do-overs to strong men, least of all *you*. So let that be the one tradition of theirs I'll keep."

"I want you to know something." My voice wheezes as he sets me on the ground.

"Make it quick. Last words with your last breath, you pesky little dragonfly."

"I know why you look so grotesque now." A burst of gold and purple spills across my eyes, the ugly shimmer of his dream, one made in a still-pure child's mind. "You didn't mean to be. You were gonna be the most beautiful boy with immortal skin ever. But then you trapped all those wailing nightmares, and their weeping dripped right onto you. And there it stays, like saggy coats of paint." His talons dig into my neck tighter.

"But I still forgive you for taking Cherie."

His grip loosens, but his eyes narrow. "He wastes the very last breath on self-righteous absolution."

"I *don't* forgive you."

I smile as I hear Alana's voice. Blood splatters my face as an arrow pierces the sandman's neck. I'm released from his grip as he falls from the giant eagle's head and collapses on the icy ground.

When he turns, Alana comes into view, the charcoal glyph on her forehead wiped away with her fingertips. Her eyes glow with silver fire, and another shaft flies from her bow and pierces through his body, this time erupting from his back and whizzing above me, landing deep in the rotted wood of the silo.

The shimmering fibers of the thunderbird's feathers are fletched on the nock, teeming with veins of electricity. Another arrow joins it, this time carrying a shriveled heart covered in dark purple bruises and bumps.

Eagle-eyed precision.

The False Eldest reels and falls to his knees in front of me, and I scramble away from him until my back touches the sturdy frame of the silo. I look up, and the pulsing arrows are sending veins of silver mist throughout the structure.

Then, the elder brothers leap from the paintings, from matte one dimension to physical forms on the ground. Eagles. Water-panthers. Moose. Wolves. Bears. A shoal of fish, all bigger than a truck, with scales rough and rigid with age.

False Eldest.

The stone-headed thunderbird from the mountain descends. The bloody-eyed eagle head that the sandman rode looks upward and whimpers.

You have put off your mountain journey for far too long.

The true elder brothers of the Ojibwe rip the sandman's skin apart. It tears away so easily, like old, worn dollar bills. I turn away.

When the ripping and gnashing subsides, I open my eyes. The elder brothers run into the sky, fading away easy as mist. In a pile of brown and red bits of flesh, there is a petite young man's body covered in a layer of ice. In his hands is a broken toy bow. Alana strides forward and stomps on the boy's frozen face.

The ice cracks, and his flesh melds tight to his bones until his gaunt frame sinks through the snow and into the dirt.

The thunderbird cradles its severed head in its wings and then reattaches it to the neck stump. Now two-headed, with numerous sets of wings, it floats above me and Alana and looks down in approval.

Countless journeys over the Fourth Hill can be finished thanks to your efforts. If there is anything you would ask, this one will grant it.

Alana walks to the door of the silo, which has been broken in and boarded up after. "He took Cherie and my son from me. I'd like to go back. I need to go back."

And you, Nameless Boy?

I smile, half tempted to ask for another spirit name. "I lost a few months of my life to that evil spirit. My family might be worried about me. If I can, I'd like to go back so they won't have to be."

The thunderbird bows both heads to us. *The power of the sacred silent guardian will take care of you both if you trust him.* Then the bird hovers down toward me, and the living head's beak nuzzles against the side of my face. *Miigwech, oshki-ogichidaag.*

Alana grabs my hand and pulls me to the silo's door. She wrenches the boards away from the frame and opens it. We take one last look at each other, no idea what lies beyond the threshold.

"What are you gonna do when you get back?" she asks. "Still gonna leave the reservation?"

"Maybe. I guess I'll go down to one of them rich casinos. I hear their blackjack tips pay well."

We laugh.

"Better than you'd ever find up here."

Ah, the casino . . .

I look back to the thunderbird. The words come from the new stone head.

I see the memories of the False Eldest from when my soul was bound as his steed. It's a place where our people gather. Worry not, for it will be under my protection from now on.

Before I can reply, Alana pulls me through the door, and the walls of the silo spin, faster and faster until the blood rushes to my head and one last vision of darkness overtakes.

Chapter 23 ☠ OUTSIDE THE SILO

ALANA BULLHEAD

November 10, 2017

When she crawled out of the snow-covered ashes of the silo, through the broken frame where the door once was, Alana pulled her phone out of her jacket pocket.

Cherie answered on the first ring. She was with Zach at the casino, as she was always supposed to be.

Alana could feel her senses realign with the return of the *jichaag*, a feeling so sharp and brilliant it shielded her from the winter air with mere thought of the sacred sevenfire, gift of the unwronged prophet.

Her child's heartbeat and kicks were alive and well. The flames let her know that he was sleeping softly, and dreaming.

Even under the sickly, orange glow that emanated from the town of Geshig, she could see the stars of the Winter Maker, whose spirit aura glowed soft blue on the edge of the sky.

Then she got in her car and returned to Atlantis.

Chapter 24 ☠ ABOARD THE BINGO BUS

MARION LAFOURNIER

November 10, 2017

The casino in Geshig is only a three-mile walk from the silo. When I step out and see daylight again, the November wind is biting yet more comfortable than any winter chill I've felt.

A friendly bus driver named Bobby Jason picks up a group of patrons, including me, at the front entrance. The loudspeaker on the atrium announces, "Last call for Hidden Atlantis!"

Bobby Jason is rowdy and raucous from the moment the van doors open, but none of the old ladies mind. They actually seem quite fond of him. He's like many older cousins and older siblings of friends I've known over the years. Dark hoodie, an urban affect to his voice, but still that characteristic rez accent, that boisterous *nehhh* after every joke. Sounds of this land that make it feel like home.

I sit in the back like a ghost and watch as someone else brings me south. But not for too long.

About forty minutes later, his van rounds the corner at Hidden Atlantis, and I see my car is right where I left it. The white pigeons scatter above us as the van reaches the drop-off site under the atrium.

On a normal day, if I was using the casino buses to ride-hop across the rez, I'd walk inside the casino, get a free soda or coffee, maybe even play a reel or two. The big golden building looks just as inviting as it did when I first arrived here, and I don't even know how to think about when that was. However long, the sandman got away with my confidence, and I feel more risk-averse than ever.

I get into my car and turn over the ignition, and when I'm safely out of sight of the casino's parking lot cameras and onto the highway, I open my Altoids container.

Five neatly rolled joints. Enough for the trip to my new home down south.

Epilogue SECUNDILUVIAN PLANS

LIAM HALTSTORM
April 1, 2018

A full shift was easy now, even though he needed a steady diet of sugar-free hard candies and ibuprofen to stem the migraines and the jitters. Almost a half year of hard work and good attendance had earned him a few shifts as a backup supervisor, and he might be well on his way to a formal promotion soon.

Around two, two buses from Canada arrived and brought in a big crowd of elderly tourists, who joined the growing casino bustle. Business usually picked up as the winter ended and the first signs of spring were in the air. Outside in the tree branches, he saw a group of crows gathering, and it spoke of a new warmth to arrive soon. When the birds returned, business boomed.

The previous night, Liam had experienced another of the nightmares that visited him regularly while trying to kick the nicotine cravings. Most nights these were the abstract, heartbeat-constricting type that led him to wake several times in a cold sweat.

But this one was different. In it he ran into Zach again, just as gaunt and pitiful as he'd last been on the banks of

Noddingham. But there was a warmth in his eyes when he looked at Liam. The warmth of a familial hug, of love and overwhelming affection.

"Brother," Zach said. "Brother again. I talked to Alana. We're getting back together! We're gonna be a family again."

"Again? But the baby."

"She's bringing him back to me. I don't know where she is, but she said she'd bring him back."

"Gee, that's great, buddy." Liam grabbed him on the shoulder.

This wretched dream-form of Zach peered into Liam's own gaze—cotton-candy-pink whites surrounding those baby blues, but caused by a sugar much less sweet. Even through the dream, he could feel the ghost of a thousand itchy corneas, times he would use the pills to stop eating for days at a time. "Someone's been singing to me, Liam. Like children on the playground, with evil smiles . . . but I know Alana can stop him." Zach took a deep breath in through his nose. "Is that nicotine craving I smell on you? It's okay, Alana said you can have a smoke break with me."

Liam woke when Zach brought a silver lighter to his face and lit the flame right beneath his eyes.

*

For the first half of his shift, his eyes still burned, no matter how many drops he used to ease the fiery itch.

Feels like that lanky jerk really put the flame in my eyes.

He paused.

What was it that Alana called her gift? Too many months of sobriety to remember.

Sevenfire sight?

The moment it came back to him, the air on the casino floor felt heavier.

When he looked across the casino, he could see a swirl of dark figures looming around the keno section. They were translucent gray humans in all manner of dress. Men in old business suits. Old ladies in big, flowery coats. Ojibwe men and women in regalia. All dancing up and around the keno section, a horrifying pow-wow of the damned. They moaned and wailed and wept and laughed.

He felt the burning rush in his eyes and remembered what Alana used to say about the Bullhead women. Their gift of sevenfire power in exchange for weaker eyesight. The reason so many in the family had those dark brown glasses that shielded their sensitive eyes from the light. He looked up at the golden canvas ceiling of Atlantis, and the lights made his eyes wince and flood with tears.

Liam fled from the infernal dance at the keno section and rushed away from the casino floor, but everywhere he turned the shapes were still flooding, extending their intangible grip on every chair, every patron, and all with their ghostly eyes focused on one thing. The slot machine screens.

His heart felt as if it could split in half as easily as an overripe peach. Everything Alana claimed that he'd dismissed since growing sober, it was all true. But what could be done?

When he backed off the soft carpeting of the casino floor, he felt his feet touch the rough tiles of the food court, where a big mural of Poseidon serving pizza on his trident hung above the cashier's station. AMBROSIA OF THE GODS read the restaurant's name in neoclassical Greek font. The fish half of Poseidon was hidden by a golden chariot drawn by seahorses, all on top of a large tidal wave.

Liam wasted no time.

"Five extra-large pies, please," he said to the cashier.

"What kind of toppings?"

"Um. It doesn't matter. Sausage. Pepperoni. Surprise me. Mix it up."

He paid for the order out of pocket and waited anxiously at one of the food court booths. He pulled out his phone, texting his direct supervisor he'd be on a lunch break until further notice and would talk to him about it later.

It was the sort of thing that might not fly on any other day, but he made sure to send it with enough vague urgency that it might avoid scrutiny.

Forty minutes later, Liam picked up the five hot, greasy boxes and tried to walk as inconspicuously as possible as he brought them to the hydraulics room.

Years ago, his first job with Hidden Atlantis was as a hotel housekeeper, and when he turned eighteen, he was allowed to transfer to the water park maintenance crew. The assaulting smell of bleach overpowered the savory pizza scent as he walked into his old department.

"Surprise gift from the higher-ups, boys," he shouted to the crew. It was a group of about ten men, excluding the dozens of lifeguards who stood vigilant beyond sight at the edge of the wave pool.

"What's the occasion?" the manager said as he helped Liam spread the boxes out onto a spare table.

"Something about the hard work for the reopening season." Because of the cost of the lavish water park, management wanted the winter closing season to be as short as possible, and to them, March was basically spring already.

When the men excitedly ripped into the boxes of pizza, Liam crept away from them, heart on fire with fear they might notice, and then he locked himself inside the hydraulic motor room.

At the control panel, he set the system power to max. Four heavy-duty levers pushed four tall metal panels in a cistern of water over and over to build up waves. Normally, it would send them out in a repeating pattern, two six-foot waves and then one ten-footer, to a crowd of water-mad swimmers.

The levers pumped the plates faster and harder until the cistern was crashing up and around, splashing his guard uniform with bleach water.

Outside the door, angry voices screamed and shouted for him to open up, but he stood stock still while the plates sent a giant wave across the park. From there, the water would flood out of the park's entrance, out into the first hotel hallway and then straight out onto the casino floor.

Liam's heart sank as he remembered how many older patrons they had on any given day and the flood of new ones that had just come in on the bus. If anyone was hurt, he would face so much trouble.

But he remembered the writhing, ugly shapes who were dancing all over, the nodding, hobbled shapes of customers at the slot machines and knew there were already so many who hurt.

What were a few more if it meant the evacuation of Atlantis?

A Native American Burial Ground Was Found Underneath A Native American Casino. Yes, You Read That Right.

by Glenn Nielan

In what some are calling the failure of the century, the Languille Lake tribe is scrambling for damage control, even reportedly hiring a PR firm to address the situation.

The tribe has remained tight-lipped about what caused their water park's wave machine to malfunction, but the rumor mill in the immediate aftermath pointed to simple employee negligence.

Thankfully, there were no major injuries when a nearly two-foot wave overtook the Hidden Atlantis casino floor, though I'm told there were a lot of purses full of cash and smart phones washed away that still haven't turned up.

What happened next will shock you.

The foundation under the keno section caved in as the water soaked into the ground, and during the excavation of the machines from the small hole, fragments of human bones were found.

In a statement released by the band after the rumors first started circulating in a local Facebook group, they declared that a small number of bones have been found and determined to be of tribal descent. They've assured the public that the remains have been moved and laid to rest, with new ceremonial rites performed to ensure rest of the wayward spirits.

Naturally, the internet wasted no time in doing what it does and making a mockery of the tribe who built a casino on their own Indian burial ground. So far, members of the council appear to be taking their roasting in stride. At a press conference, recently elected Tribal President Makwade Binesi-Smith was quoted as saying, "It's been a little embarrassing for all, but profits have been up at our other sites since the internet traffic."

When asked if they would be reviewing other sites for similar issues, Binesi-Smith dismissed the idea. "Look, if you dig anywhere, chances are, you're gonna find bones."

The writer of this article has contacted the tribe for comment but has not yet received a response.

This old man,

He played; won

Acknowledgments

This book would not have been possible through the last five years without the encouragement and patience of my family and friends, and the dedication and help of my agent, Eleanor, my editor, Harry, and all the staff at Counterpoint Press.

Thank you to the Indigenous writers who help each other stay dedicated and excited to our literary landscape. Thank you to Linda LeGarde Grover for your dedication and spirit as a professor and mentor during uncertain times. A special thanks as always to Tommy Orange, Terese Marie Mailhot, Derek Palacio, Claire Vaye Watkins, Pam Houston, Ramona Ausubel, and Marie-Helene Bertino, Kim Blaeser, and David Tromblay.

A giant, heartfelt thank-you to any past coworker of mine.

DENNIS E. STAPLES is an Ojibwe writer from Bemidji, Minnesota, and the author of *This Town Sleeps*. He holds an MFA in fiction from the Institute of American Indian Arts and is a graduate of the 2018 Clarion West Writers Workshop and a recipient of the Octavia E. Butler Memorial Scholarship. His work has appeared in *Asimov's Science Fiction* and *Nightmare* magazine. He is a member of the Red Lake Nation.